Burning with Desire

Burning with Desire

A Men of Marietta Romance

Patricia W. Fischer

TULE
PUBLISHING

Burning with Desire
Copyright © 2017 Patricia W. Fischer
Tule Publishing First Printing, April 2017

The Tule Publishing Group, LLC

ALL RIGHTS RESERVED

No part of this book may be used or reproduced in any manner whatsoever without written permission except in the case of brief quotations embodied in critical articles and reviews.

This is a work of fiction. Names, characters, places, and incidents are products of the author's imagination or are used fictitiously. Any resemblance to actual events, locales, organizations, or persons, living or dead, is entirely coincidental.

ISBN: 978-1-946772-55-8

Hello Readers,

I am thrilled for you to read my first book with Tule Publishing and to be a part of the Montana Born series.

Gabriella and Kyle were so much fun to write. Their passion and their humor made for a great project and one I hope you'll enjoy.

As always, there's a journey I take as an author and there are a few people I want to thank for helping me get here.

First, Teri Wilson, who told me if I didn't submit, she'd kick my butt until I did. Extra unicorns, rainbows, and glitter for you, my friend.

Second, my husband. Thank you for accepting the fact that I'm not a great housekeeper and don't keep up with the laundry.

Third, my children. Thank you for doing the laundry.

Fourth, to my amazing writer peeps at San Antonio Romance Authors. Without y'all, I'd still be wondering how to be a full-time writer.

Have fun. Enjoy the book and let me know what you think. *Ciao!*

Chapter One

WHY DID I immediately agree to move to the middle of nowhere?

The chilly air slapped her through the slightly open window as she forced herself to stay awake. Gabriella Marcos rolled her head from side to side, hoping to work the kinks out.

Four days in the car would soon end with them starting a new life in one of the last places on Earth she ever thought they'd be.

Marietta, Montana.

She had struggled to stay focused while driving the last several hours in pitch dark, but Gabriella convinced herself it would be worth it for them to push through. Get to their new house.

Put some distance between them and family.

The first breaths of morning light peeked over the snow-covered mountains.

Despite her exhaustion, she stared at the sight in awe, taking in the jagged outline of white caps for the first time.

"Not much of that in Texas." She sighed as butterflies

danced in her stomach. Her anxiety stalled in overdrive.

Or was that hunger?

She finished off the last drops of the two large rotgut coffees she'd purchased in Sheridan when they'd filled up last time. Tossing the cup in the large fast-food bag that sat in the front passenger seat, Gabriella reviewed what she'd have to get ready by this Monday when she officially met her new employees for the first time.

The gas tank light flashed low, which meant her fuel would last her no more than twenty miles. Not great for pulling a U-Haul trailer in hard side winds.

Glancing at the dashboard clock, she cringed at the early hour, knowing there would be no gas station open or a bathroom until they got to Marietta.

Should've filled up again in Billings. Why is my organizational clock so off?

When the answer popped in her head, it was all she could do not to crack a tooth from stress.

I'm doing the right thing. I'm protecting my family.

The pile of blankets in the backseat hadn't moved in a bit.

All my family.

She repositioned herself in her seat and tried to shake off the fatigue that settled deep in her bones.

Great way to start out, Gabby. Stranded. No one to call. Needing to pee.

The idea of exposing her bare skin on the side of the road didn't bother her. Growing up in the Texas Hill Country, she'd done her share of fertilizing the ground. It was what the outside temperature gauge blinked that more than got her attention.

Twenty-seven degrees? Good grief, it's the end of March! What have I done?

She white-knuckled the wheel as her mind raced with self-doubt at the monumental risk she'd taken. Moving here considering Gabriella had never been—much less lived—outside of Texas was one thing, but to buy a diner sight unseen?

All because of one bad boss, his tyrannical daughter, and an even worse fiancé.

Her rational brain corrected. *Ex-fiancé.*

Shivering from the cold whooshing around her, she closed the window, but turned the heat to low. The threadbare sweater she'd purchased long ago sat loosely on her body, giving her little protection from the frigid temperatures.

I couldn't keep working there.

Tears pricked the backs of her eyelids at her decision.

Five years of my life tossed because I had to stay quiet.

She rubbed the back of her neck as exhaustion tried to creep in, lull her to sleep.

This is better for us, right? In Marietta, I get to be my own boss. Trinity gets to start over with school.

Worry began to squelch excitement, but then she remembered her precious recipe books on the floorboard in front of the passenger seat. Replaying the ingredients of her beloved *Brownies Picantes*, plus multiple other culinary delights, helped a slow calm subdue the anxiety.

Those perfect chocolaty treats had won Paige Sheenan over, which led to her suggesting Gabriella buy Main Street Diner, which led to them driving in freezing weather and in dire need of a bathroom.

It's gonna be okay. I made the right choice for us. For her. Right?

Glancing in the rearview mirror, she realized that the pile of blankets hadn't moved since they'd stopped in Wyoming around two.

Somewhere in that pile slept Trinity, along with Belle and Cookie, two of the most high-maintenance animals Gabriella had ever owned.

Of course, raising a teenager hadn't been a walk in the park, either. Recently her daughter had proven to be a challenge. Her sweet-natured child had morphed into a moody, frustrated, and anxious girl.

It's because of all the bullying. It'll be better here. She'll be better here.

But Gabriella couldn't be completely sure of that.

Unexpected tears started to fall at the memory of her late best friend, Laurie, who was Trinity's bio mother.

Laurie was a handful right about this age. Lord help me if she starts to act like her.

Shaking off her worry, she focused on the road and her passengers.

At least they all traveled well and her daughter more than

supported the move out of Lone Star Crossing.

A loud snore echoed from the backseat, making Gabriella giggle. *Belle needs a Breathe Right strip. Poor old dog.*

Apparently, the vibrations of the snore woke Cookie the cat. She jumped between the front seats, stretched, gave Gabriella a *Jeez, we're not there yet?* look, before gingerly hopping into the oversized fast-food paper bag in the passenger seat. After finding her footing among the trash, she poked her head out. Her crystal-blue eyes sat just above the bag's edge as she scanned the world whipping by.

"What do you think, Cookie? You ready for a new adventure?" Of course, the deaf cat didn't answer but continued to stare out the window with wide-eyed wonder.

Gabriella scratched the feline behind the ears.

Immediately, Cookie purred.

The reflective sign up ahead proclaimed that they were about to cross over into Crawford County and noted the short distance to Marietta. "We're gonna make it."

With a flick of her wrist, Gabriella turned off the heater, hoping it would help extend the precious drops of gas she had left as the last digital fuel line blinked.

About fifteen miles.

She knew her daughter, dog, and cat could keep each other warm during this last stretch. The cold would more than keep her focused and awake, but that didn't solve all her problems.

What I wouldn't give for a bathroom right now.

Within minutes, the sky had lightened from its midnight-blue to a deep-sea azure.

Off to the side of the road stood a stake with a large wreath hanging on it. The white ribbon across it said, "Harry."

Oh, how sad. I wonder what happened?

As she wondered, the town of Marietta came into view.

She breathed a sigh of relief as they slowed at the first stoplight and turned right onto Main Street. A gas station sat off to her right, but its lights were dimmed.

At least I know where it is.

Pockets of snow lay scattered under trees and in corners of the deserted high school parking lot. Glancing at the clock above her digital map, her brow furrowed.

No one there. Is it spring break?

The Main Street store lights reminded her of an airport runway, lights flashing as if to guide her along the straight path to the impressive courthouse at the end of the street.

A law office here, a chocolate shop next to the flower shop across from a bookstore there.

This looks wonderful. Very Capraesque.

Despite her need for relief and no one driving behind her, she lingered at the last stop sign to catch a quick glimpse of the Main Street Diner.

Through the front picture window, Gabriella beamed as three waitresses gracefully navigated the packed house, tables, and chairs while holding pots of coffee.

Pride filled her chest.

That's my place.

She wondered what it would look like in the summer when the rich chocolate and special spices of her *Brownies Picantes* were in the air. Or at Christmas when the smell of cinnamon, nutmeg, and sugar from her *Alfajores* cookies would float out the door and beckon people inside.

To my diner.

A quick honk pulled her out of her reverie. Making a left, she turned on Court until it bent into Bramble Lane, past the large Victorian-style home with a Bramble House Bed and Breakfast sign out front.

Past the park and the multiple oak and pine trees that lined the street until finally, near the end of the street, sat her house. A sweet little two-story bungalow home with a front porch and small fenced-in yard. It even had a white picket fence that was in desperate need of repainting.

Save that project for the spring.

Glancing at the temperature reading again, she corrected herself.

Late spring.

Even with so many at her busy café, it appeared most of the town still slept and many front porch lights glowed.

Off in the distance, she could just make out the edge of the school's athletic track and the uprights.

We drove in a big U. Easy enough.

A few cars pulled into the school's parking lot. *Guess it's not spring break.*

The house next door's front room and upstairs lights

were on, but the house they'd rented sat dark. She double-checked the address and sure enough, she'd gotten them here in one piece.

Shaking off her worry once she put the car in park, Gabriella let out a long breath.

We made it—Mama will be so unhappy to hear.

The last words her overprotective mother said to her before they drove away were, "I don't know why I'm saying goodbye. You won't make it out of Texas before you turn around and come home just like you always have."

As soon as they'd crossed the state line into New Mexico, her mother called incessantly, wondering when they were going to head home. Angelica Marcos could guilt with the best of them and that guilt was laid on like heavy cream for every state line they passed.

But you're here now. You did it. Gabriella held on to that nugget of pride. So far, she'd even proven herself wrong.

As best she could tell, Marietta looked about half the size of her beloved Lone Star Crossing, but she'd get a better idea during daylight hours after she'd had a good nap, and visited a bathroom.

A wadded-up piece of paper came flying out of the food bag and, following it, the cat frantically attempted to juggle the ball of trash. Cookie and the paper ended up on the floorboard of the passenger seat as she batted it around and knocked it into the box of recipe books.

The outside temperature gauge blinked twenty-five. *Great.*

The thin sweater Gabriella wore didn't look like near enough layering in the Montana spring.

The winds gently rocked the car. She eyed the front door, wondering if she'd freeze to death before getting them inside.

Trinity and Belle were still snuggled in and appeared to be sleeping.

After wrapping the sweater tightly around her body, she grabbed her purse, and counted to three before opening the door.

The cold winds slapped at her face and sucked the air out of her lungs.

Ay Dios mio!

She dashed for the door and lifted the corner of the mat to find…nothing.

What?

She yanked the entire thing off the ground to find…nothing.

No. No. No.

Shifting her weight frantically, she knew if she didn't find a toilet soon, she'd make one awful first impression on her neighbors. *And then probably freeze to death.*

Scanning the porch, she didn't see anywhere else the key would be tucked.

Maybe it's under the back-door mat?

A brisk wind penetrated her light sweater and shot a chill into her bones.

Fine. Back door it is.

Chapter Two

THE STEADY BEAT of his runs had always been great comfort for Kyle Cavasos. Ever since his basketball and track days, as well as during his military training, the solitude of his own workouts helped him focus and mentally decompress from his insane family life.

After a restless night's sleep, he'd woken early and hit the treadmill. For the past hour, he'd run, staring at the black of the night as it changed into the rich blue of morning and the stars faded. Within the past few minutes, the vivid oranges and yellows spread out over Copper Mountain range like hot caramel over vanilla ice cream.

His anxiety calmed watching the golden flecks of sun glisten in the snow as Mumford & Sons finished up "Lover of the Light" on his iPhone.

When he moved in months ago, he'd set up his treadmill facing out of the upstairs window of his small house because it had the perfect view of the mountains. No matter the weather, he could run and think of nothing other than climbing those hills and getting away from everything. Which was one of the many reasons he moved to Marietta after he'd fulfilled his military obligation. To stay as far away from the chaos his movie producer/hotel mogul mother and celebrity siblings willingly created.

And I don't want anything to do with…him.

Sweat poured off his brow and stung his eyes. He shook off the pain and cranked up the speed.

Get out of my head.

Every day, he'd work out to the point of exhaustion to keep his center.

Every day, he'd erase the family baggage by sweating out his frustrations.

And every day, he thanked the blue heavens he wasn't anything like his father.

My bio father.

But today, the workout hadn't done anything to quell his growing anger over the latest issue of *US Weekly* that sat on his kitchen table.

Dammit, Jason, can't you keep it in your pants for five minutes?

He yanked the emergency cord out of the treadmill before the first verse of the Dave Matthews Band's "Crash into Me" could finish. With his heart pounding in his ears, he collapsed in the oversized leather chair and dried his face with his shirt.

At least the paparazzi haven't found me yet.

How long would that last? Kyle knew it would only be a matter of time before that beast would come knocking on his door. One viral social media post would completely blow his cover and he'd have to face reality.

He'd already taken a chance by posing for that First Responder calendar. The proofs sat on the kitchen table with the rest of his mail. *Nice that Charlie let me hide part of my face with the fireman helmet.*

His back itched thinking about lying shirtless on that bale of hay for the long photo shoot.

That's what I get for being October.

At least he hadn't been asked to strategically place a pumpkin. It was bad enough the photographer, Charlie Foster, and her friends successfully convinced all the men posing to get their chests waxed, much less to worry about a picture showing him provocatively positioning a squash.

How ironic the Brit thought he was a natural in front of her camera.

If she only knew how many times I've had to pose and pretend to be someone else.

Drying his face again, he rested his elbows on his knees and stared mindlessly out the window.

But it was for a good cause, right? For Harry.

His heart sat heavy when he remembered the first guy who welcomed him to the fire department last summer. Harry Monroe acted as tour guide for the first month, introducing Kyle to everyone in town, showing him the best fishing spots, the best trails to hike, the perfect places to sit in the quiet.

After being raised in the wealth and opulence of high society and its backstabbing ways, Kyle loved the calmness of this place and the special memories it held.

Years ago, Patrick, Kyle's father, and he had spent their last father-son ski vacation in Marietta before his dad got sick.

On the table next to him sat a picture of that very trip. He grabbed the frame and smiled at the memories of that day.

Even coming back here twenty years later, Kyle loved the fact the town hadn't changed much. And he appreciated the people more. The long-time residents were solid, salt of the Earth folks who told it like they saw it, but were always there to lend a hand, even if they didn't always agree with you.

Like Harry.

It didn't seem fair. Even after serving in the Navy and treating his share of battlefield wounded, Kyle had yet to understand how so many lives never played out. Why certain people lived and others died. Especially when some of those men as good as Harry didn't get their happily ever after.

Kyle would never forget the last conversation he had with his friend, right before Harry told him he was stopping to help a couple on the side of the road.

And just like that. He was gone.

Sweat ran down Kyle's face as his pulse returned to normal before he remembered the chaos his bio dad had caused once again.

Glancing up at the Navy corpsman shadow box, his diploma from UCLA, his certification of completion from the

Marietta Fire Department, his national firefighter certification, he shook his head. Out of all the things he'd accomplished in his life, it angered him beyond reason that as far as pop culture was concerned, he would never be more than a Hollywood scandal.

No matter what I do, I'm always gonna be his kid. Her kid.

Despite his anger, he gently placed the picture back on the table. "Miss you, Dad."

He rubbed his temples and tried to shake off his annoyance before noticing the photo tucked in the edge of frame of his fire department certification.

Harry smiled back at him.

He'd be mad at me feeling sorry for myself.

Glancing at his father's face again, Kyle smirked. "So would you."

For the next several minutes, Kyle simply watched the sunrise. Listened to the wind as it beat the bare branches of the two oak trees in his yard. Small remaining bits of snow on the windowpane flew off and danced with the gusts.

Exhaustion crept in and he considered returning to bed, but knew he had to stay up to give the key to the new neighbor moving in next door.

I hope whoever that is will keep to themselves.

The rich smell of Colombia's best drifted across the house like a siren, beckoning him into the kitchen.

Come on. Get up. Get moving.

The instructions sounded a lot like Harry.

Kyle smirked and headed downstairs and toward the

back of the house.

He weaved around the boxes of clothes he'd gotten his sister, Meredith, to collect at her gallery. They were ready to anonymously donate to the child and teen center in Harry's name.

Since no one ever came over, Kyle kept the boxes in his living room.

A thick Burberry red sweater fell on the floor as he brushed by. As he picked it up, he cringed at the labels. Kate Spade. Dolce & Gabbana. Ralph Lauren. Prada.

Dammit, Meredith. Couldn't you have gotten donations from normal people? Walking in with three boxes of designer clothes would certainly raise a few eyebrows in town. Especially since Kyle had said little about his family and had never mentioned his famous parents.

As far as anyone here was concerned, he was a retired Navy corpsman, now paramedic and firefighter, who visited the area years before and decided to come back and stay.

No one knew any better. No one other than Harry.

Gently he folded the sweater and placed it on top of the pile.

As the coffee brewed at the same time it always did, he picked up the scandal magazine that had caused him so much distress. On the cover stood movie star and his bio dad, Jason Crowe, in a too-small Speedo kissing his latest costar. The woman, probably a good twenty-five years his junior, wore something that covered her about as well as strings of dental floss.

On his father's left hand, was his most recent wedding ring that still had the shine from his wedding day not two months ago.

Kyle grit his teeth so hard it hurt.

Jason Crowe has cheated on every other wife and girlfriend he's had. I don't know why anyone thinks this is news.

Disgusted, Kyle tossed the magazine on top of the ripped-up manila envelope it came in. A large stack of documents fluttered as the magazine produced a small gust of air upon landing. Since yesterday, he'd chosen to ignore what had arrived in that envelope, but today he'd have to address it. His mother's deadline had arrived.

That frustrated him just as much as Jason's blatant infidelities.

Filling up his oversized US Navy mug with his favorite drink, he breathed in the goodness, hoping the caffeine would put him in a better mood.

He needed to get out of this funk. He needed a good breakfast at the Main Street Diner, a good book, and…

"Are those legs?"

A long pair of legs wiggled frantically and disappeared into the house next door.

Damn kids.

Without bothering to grab a jacket, Kyle scooped up the house keys left by next door's owner and took off.

After running up the front steps, he unlocked the door

and raced into pitch darkness and a bitter cold.

Cheap asses. Keep it freezing to save money.

His heart beat hard in his ears, making it difficult to listen for footsteps.

Nothing.

Walking as quietly as the hardwood floors would allow, Kyle finally noticed one room with a light coming out from underneath the door.

Without thought, he grabbed the doorknob, yanked the door open, and came face to face with the intruder...as she used the bathroom.

Chapter Three

A MAN SUDDENLY appeared in the doorway.
"Are you kidding me?" Gabriella screamed and held her sweater up to her shoulders, completely covering herself.

"What are you doing in here?"

"I'm testing the pipes for basilisks before I rent it," she snapped incredulously. "What do you think I'm doing?"

As if it finally registered where she was sitting, his eyebrows hit his hairline. A nervous laugh escaped him as he looked everywhere but at her. "Holy shit. Sorry. So sorry."

"Now get out! Get out! I'll talk to you in a minute!"

He held his hands up in surrender and backed out, closing the door with his foot.

Once the stranger left and her heart rate returned to normal, Gabriella tried to laugh at the ridiculousness of it all. Only tears of exhaustion fell.

How did I get all the way here without a hitch and then this happens? Being caught on the toilet?

If the drive back to Texas hadn't been almost twenty-four straight hours, if she'd slept for more than six hours in the past two days, and if she wouldn't have to hear her mother say "I told you so" for the rest of her life, Gabriella would have seriously considered getting in the car and heading home.

She shook off her embarrassment.

It's a minor setback. Woman up!

After she cleaned up, Gabriella took a few deep breaths, held her shoulders back, and walked into the frigid wall of air. *"Virgen Santa!"*

A choked laugh from the stranger as he held his hand in front of his face. "You okay?"

His deep voice tickled her ears and unexpectedly set her wonderfully off center as she sat in one of the kitchen chairs. "Good grief. It's like Antarctica."

"It'll get warm in a minute." His deep blue military sweatshirt perfectly outlined his broad shoulders.

"Why do they keep it so cold in here? Were you wearing that a minute ago?"

"Probably to save on heating bills. Not many people renting this time of year." He extended his hand. "I'm Kyle. Cavasos. I live next door."

It suddenly occurred to her that this guy looked like a pinup model. Her embarrassment waned as a hot flash rolled over her and settled south of her belly button.

Hell-o, neighbor. She responded in kind, trying not to giggle like some fangirl. "Marcos. Gabriella. Marcos."

"Then that would make you double O what?"

He knows movies, then. "Twenty-nine. My age. Nope,

I'm not an MI6 agent."

"I am sorry to bust in on you. Since spring break some of the kids in the area haven't been acting all that great. Guess they're getting cabin fever. Thought they were using the house to party." He ran his fingers through his thick head of honey-colored hair. "The owner said they told you to come get the key from me."

"They were supposed to leave the keys under the front doormat." She nonchalantly shrugged in her attempt to remain casual despite the fact part of her brain had turned into a gooey pile of giggles. *My gosh, he's gorgeous.*

"They left town yesterday for a family emergency. Told me they emailed you." The morning light shone through the kitchen window, highlighting the scruff on his chin.

Lawd-y, Montana grows them nice. "I haven't had the greatest cell service since we left Fort Collins."

Really, I've been avoiding checking my emails.

A loud rumble echoed through the house, making the floor vibrate a few seconds. She jumped to her feet. "What's that?"

"It's the heater. I turned it up since the owner had it set on sixty."

A thick band of snow sat along the backyard windowsill. "This will take some getting used to."

"What? The house?"

"No, the cold." Pulling her oversized wisp of a sweater tightly around her, she shivered. "It's freezing. I mean bone-chilling cold."

"I can help you with that."

Reeeeeally? I just bet you can, mister.

He shifted to his left. On the counter sat a large coffee mug with steam rising out of it. "When I grabbed my hoodie I got this for you. I hope you like coffee."

If he hadn't just seen her in a most compromising position, she might have kissed him. Still, when she noticed what was on the mug, if he'd proposed, she would have seriously considered it. "Is that a map mug from…from Harry Potter?"

"You know, since you were checking for basilisks and all." A slight color of crimson washed across his cheeks.

He's literate. He's funny. He's hot. Marietta is awesome.

Maybe the exhaustion had yanked her defenses down.

Maybe Gabriella simply appreciated that someone else in this world had finally taken the time to do something nice for her. Or maybe after having to deal with an adulterous ex-fiancé and a recipe-stealing boss, a nice guy looked…well, nice.

And this guy looked *very nice*.

Whatever the reason, she couldn't sway the urge to hug him.

"Thank you." Before he could hand her the coffee, she wrapped her arms around him and pulled him close. Full-on hugged him flush against her.

He smelled like vanilla and coffee. Subtly, she inhaled.

Apparently, it wasn't subtle enough.

"Just worked out. Haven't showered yet. Don't hold it against me."

"You're fine." Mentally, she cringed at his comment, but she wasn't ashamed enough to move. It was that or she was still really cold and hugging him felt like hugging a warm marshmallow.

A ripped, gorgeous, delicious-looking marshmallow.

His arms circled her as his low chuckle tickled her neck. "Guess you like coffee."

"You have no idea." She absentmindedly kissed him on the cheek as she began to pull away. "And you read."

"Have trouble finding guys who bring you coffee *and* know how to use a book?" His green eyes sparkled with mischief.

The corner of her mouth curled up at his humor. "You would be surprised how underestimated being literate is in the dating pool. It usually sits on the shallow end."

"Glad I like deep water."

"Me too." *Jeez, he's good at nerd banter.*

The more she talked to him, the less afraid she became of the unknown.

In fact, the unknown looks pretty damned good right now.

Her eyes betrayed her and focused on his full lips.

I wonder how well the unknown kisses.

The creak of the floors yanked her out of her wonder.

Kyle dropped his arms. "You expecting someone?"

The slow tap-tap-tap of nails on hardwoods approached. "*Mi dio*. I don't know where my brain is."

"Gabby, it's freezing out there." With Cookie in her arms, Trinity slunk down the hall before plopping her butt in a chair.

"I'm so sorry." Gabriella smoothed out her sweater as the realization sunk in of how she'd thrown herself at the first person she met.

Setting a great example there, Gabby. "I needed to get the key and turn the heat on. It was freezing in here."

"And you are?" Her daughter's eyes narrowed.

Kyle extended his hand. "Kyle Cavasos. I live next door."

Hesitantly, Trinity responded in kind. "What are you doing here, then?"

Oh, jeez. How do I explain this? "Kyle, he—"

"Had the key." He shrugged. "The people who own this place had to leave town yesterday. I came over when I saw your mom drive up to give her the key and help her figure out how to work the heat."

Heat indeed. The new neighbor might be covered up by a bulky hoodie, but sneaking a peek at his long, muscular legs, Gabby might have to fan herself at the other muscles she could only imagine.

When she glanced up, his eyes locked with hers.

The corner of his full lips curled slightly, making this a total panty-melting moment.

Does Montana have some secret air pheromones that blow

off the mountain in springtime? "Um, yes, he brought the key over and here we all are."

"Don't forget Belle." Trinity pointed.

Kyle's eyebrow cocked. "Belle?"

Belle sleepily walked in behind, her nails hitting the floor in a slow, steady beat. The old Lab circled Trinity's chair and flopped down next to one of the floor vents. The warm airstream immediately blew up some of her loose fur and catapulted the dark strands across the linoleum.

Kyle tilted his head toward the front of the house. "Anyone else I should expect?"

"You're asking if I'm married? Nope, this is all of us." Gabriella realized she'd been twisting a lock of hair between her fingers. *Good grief. Quit acting like you're sixteen.*

"Looks like a full house." He gave her a lopsided smirk.

Tucking her hands in her jeans pockets, she agreed, "Better full than empty, right?"

Some of the playfulness faded in his eyes. "Right."

What's that about? "Kyle, this is my daughter—"

"Adopted goddaughter." The girl rolled her eyes while she continued to scratch the cat's neck. "My mom's gone."

Gabriella reined in her frustration at her daughter's rebuttal.

Ever since they'd visited Trinity's aunt a few days ago, for the first time ever, the teen had refused to call Gabriella mom.

Push through, Gabby. Push through. "This is Trinity. And

Belle and Cookie."

Kyle gave them each a nod. "Nice to meet you all."

He stepped forward and reached out to pat Cookie on the back, but Trinity pulled Cookie close to her body. "She doesn't like strangers. She can't hear so she doesn't trust too many people."

Picking up the mug, Gabriella agreed, "That is true. Cookie's not much for strangers. She's an albino, born deaf."

"Ah, that explains the blue eyes and white fur." He backed away, his hands up in surrender. "Fair enough. I'll let Cookie alone."

A look of *Are you kidding me? He's beautiful!* flashed across the feline's face. She pushed herself away from Trinity, sauntered across the floor, and rubbed her whiskers against Kyle's bare shin.

"Is she about to use me as a scratching post?" He nervously chuckled but remained still.

"I don't think so." A look of confusion set on Trinity's face. "That's totally weird by the way."

Cookie meowed, stood up on her hind legs, and extended her front paws like a child who wished to be picked up.

Kyle scooped the cat up in his arms. Within seconds, she snuggled in and purred loudly. A few strands of her white hair stuck to his sweatshirt.

"You're the cat whisperer." Trinity's eyes went wide with surprise.

No kidding. Gabriella had to blink twice to make sure she

saw all this correctly. Up until this moment, Cookie liked all of two people in this world and they stood in this room.

"To the cat whisperer." Gabriella toasted him before taking a healthy swig of the best coffee she'd drunk in the past two days.

Trinity motioned for Gabriella to give her the mug. "You know you're gonna have to marry this guy, right?"

Heat shot up Gabriella's nose. Frantically, she grabbed her sweater, holding it against her face. As soon as she caught her breath, she sputtered, "T!"

Her daughter gave her a sly smirk while relieving Gabriella of the cup. "Just sayin'. She never liked Peter the Cheater."

Thanks, T. Our hot new neighbor doesn't want my sad backstory. "That wasn't his name."

"Okay, she didn't like *Derrick*. Derrick, Derrick, the great big—"

"Language, please." Plastering on her best "I'm fine" smile, Gabriella turned to Kyle. "But it's all good. Ancient history."

"Glad to hear." He continued to pet the cat as she shed all over his dark blue hoodie.

"I'm gonna go find my room in this ice box. Go back to sleep." Trinity exited with the swiped mug.

"Sounds good, T."

"Check ya later, Cat Man."

He held up the peace sign. "Later, T."

Cookie jumped down and followed the teen out, leaving Kyle and Gabriella in silence.

He handed her the key before leaning toward the hallway. "I'll get going. Sounds like you two need some rest."

Disappointment settled in her gut at his impending exit. "Thank you so much for the interesting welcome. I'm sure I'll be talking to you soon."

"Glad you're talking to me after that."

"Crazy morning."

He tucked his hands in the front of his hoodie and walked with her to the front door. "You don't need help unloading?"

"Honestly, the last thing I want to do is work. We've been driving for days. I'm exhausted. I'll go out and get my herbs and plants and we'll take care of the rest of it later."

"If you're interested, there's the Main Street Diner that serves a good pot roast and a better cup of coffee than I can make. Maybe I could take you two to dinner this evening?" He cleared his throat as if he were searching for the right words. "I can drive you around a bit. Show you where things are. Grocery store. Gas station. High school."

Her heart fluttered. *Marietta is already turning out to be a great move.*

"I know where the restaurant is. Saw it when I drove in."

"Oh." His forehead furrowed.

Nice move, dimwit. "But I think a tour would be lovely. Thank you."

"Great. Seven?"

"Seven." She moved an imaginary object on the floor with her foot. "Guess I should tell you, I'm the new owner. Of the diner."

"Gabriella." His eyes went wide as if he'd remembered something. "Gabriella. Marcos. That's you."

"That's me."

"Flo told me Paige sold it."

News travels fast. "Flo is?"

"One of the waitresses there. She's been there for years." He gave her a smile that should have been illegal this early in the morning. "You from here?"

"No." She liked the way his lips moved when he looked at her.

"You have family here?"

Family. The word twisted her guts. "No."

"How did you end up buying the diner?"

"Funny story. Paige's husband's company had a retreat at the resort where I worked. I was in charge of the food. Paige liked what I made and jokingly asked if I wanted to run the diner." She cleared her throat, hoping her words came out more positive than she felt about what actually transpired. "I told her yes and here I am."

He studied her for a moment before answering. "Yes, you are. I go there a few times a week."

"Then I look forward to seeing you there. And next door."

"And this evening." He playfully shrugged.

Her cheeks hurt from grinning so broadly. Again, she twisted a lock of hair between her fingers like some teenage girl trying to be coy. *Get hold of yourself!*

His intense green eyes sent tingles all over, making her shiver in the most delicious way. It was that or the crisp chill in the air that swept in when he opened the door. "I appreciate your help this morning. Even though it was…weird."

"If you need anything, you know where to find me." He pointed toward his house.

"Got your address."

Like an awkward teen, he leaned forward and gave her a quick kiss on the cheek. "See you soon."

Yes. You absolutely will.

Chapter Four

What was I thinking?

Kyle couldn't believe he'd acted like some lovesick teen talking to his first crush, but he'd been floored with how impressively Gabriella handled herself during their first introduction.

His phone buzzed and danced across his bathroom counter.

Most women would have been too ashamed to even make eye contact after such a disastrous initial meeting. Gabriella handled it like a champ, with a solid literary comeback no less.

She'd even understood his subtle joke with the boy wizard themed mug and laughed off her embarrassment.

Kyle grit his teeth at his response to her reading reference.

Glad I like deep water.

He wiped the steam off the mirror and stared at himself.

You sounded like a dumbass.

The phone buzzed again. He refused to look at it until he got dressed, mainly because he knew who kept texting him.

As he began shaving, Gabriella's words about reading replayed in his head.

"You would be surprised how underestimated being literate is in the dating pool." Her playful banter made him smile and also wonder what kind of guys she'd been involved with.

Peter the Cheater? Her daughter's comment made him wonder if that's why she was in Marietta. To get away? Start over? Because unless you were born here or you had family here, most people weren't moving to Marietta for its stimulating nightlife and social scene.

Even the locals had their stories of leaving and coming back.

Being an outsider, he'd kept his history quiet.

Thankfully, the guys at the station didn't push him much about why he ended up here, not that he'd tell them any more than he already had.

But Gabriella and Trinity are outsiders, too. Nice to have some company.

The more he thought about it, the more he really wanted to get to know Gabriella's reason for being here; because he hoped she wouldn't have to leave anytime soon.

Once he'd dried off and finished shaving, he checked his phone after the multiple texts. Six text messages from his mother.

Not now. He tossed his phone on the bed.

Grabbing the first three shirts out of his closet, then deciding he didn't like any of them, he put them back and tried a fourth. With shaking hands, he attempted to button his clothes, but his nerves had him out of sorts.

He opened and closed his fists and tried again.

It's dinner. Not marriage. Just dinner.

But something about her yanked him to attention faster than any chief petty officer ever had. Could it be her long dark hair and cocoa skin or the fact she had smooth curves like a gently winding road? And what about the fire in her eyes when she stood up to him or her quick, smart comebacks?

He hadn't been this worked up about a woman in years. And it was nice to know she noticed him because of *him* and not his parents.

It might only be dinner, but I'd sure like to make her breakfast.

The clock read ten to seven before he'd finally layered up enough to tolerate the brisk spring evening.

He laughed as he zipped up his heavy coat. Every time he wore it, fellow first responders Dan, Gavin, and Jonah—the Clark brothers—would joke with him about the many layers he'd wear.

As longtime residents, those three could wear T-shirts and jeans when it froze outside and they'd be more than comfortable.

Only being here a year, Kyle had yet to acclimate enough to go without a heavy coat for most of the winter and spring.

The hard winds and smell in the air signaled another round of snow would blanket them by the weekend.

I wonder if those Texas ladies are ready for that.

He laughed at her trying to keep warm with that paper-thin sweater. *She's gonna need a heavy coat—and quick.*

On the counter next to the coffee pot sat a bag of groceries he'd purchased after he checked in at the firehouse this afternoon. Pulling out his Igloo bag, he loaded up a few staples to take next door.

Next, he finished the protein prep for tomorrow, which consisted of tossing a few chicken breasts into a large Ziploc bag along with his special blend of seasonings, lemon pepper and salt, and a bit of olive oil. Shaking the bag, he checked the chicken had a decent distribution of spices before burping the bag and placing it back in the refrigerator.

The phone rang as he grabbed his watch and wallet from the kitchen table. Without looking at the caller, he hit the speaker button.

"Kyle!"

Dammit. Should've looked before answering. "Mother. How's your evening?"

"Why haven't you answered my texts? I've sent you at least twenty." The harshness of Lillian Winston-Cavasos's voiced pierced the tranquility of his house. No doubt, her attempt to ruin his good mood.

"You sent six and, Mom, I'm about to head out the door. What do you need?"

A long pause, which only meant she was sucking in enough air to rant a good, long time. "What do I need? Hmm, let's see. I need you to sign those contracts, pack your things, and tell me when your start date will be."

All the documents his mother sent him were spread out on the kitchen table next to the pile of final proofs from the calendar photo shoot. At the top of each page, URGENT had been stamped right next to the Winston Enterprises Logo.

As if I'd forgotten the time frame I'm on.

Before he could answer, she added, "You promised me you'd head to Texas after you got this firefighter thing out of your system. Take over your grandfather's first resort property as he willed you to do."

"I don't have to make this decision for another six months, Mom. I'm fine where I am."

"As a fireman in nowhere town?" Her response dripped in sarcasm.

"I'm a paramedic and a fireman and I like it here."

"Well, I'm a producer and director and I like it here in LA. Doesn't mean I can throw my family's company down the toilet." She sucked in a loud breath. "There are a lot of people counting on their jobs and I'll be damned if I'll let anyone else run these places."

Probably smoking those overpriced cigarettes that are never farther than two feet from her. "I'm not telling you to sell. Just send someone else."

"I don't understand you sometimes. You asked me to

make sure the Jewel of the Hill Country Resort and Spa was in good hands until you had a year of downtime after serving...whatever you did in the military."

"I was in the Navy."

"I thought you said you were with the Marines."

"No, my title was Marine Corps Recon Foreman. The Marines don't have a medical branch. Navy covers that for them. It's confusing."

"Whatever. You said you wanted to run the property in San Antonio."

"I know." *That was before I realized the value of being invisible.*

"I gave you the year like you asked. Now, it's time to step up."

When he arrived here last summer, all he'd planned to do was work and get away from the Hollywood crazy, but he'd grown to like it. Love it here. The last place he wanted to move was, well, anywhere else. "Mom, listen—"

"No, Kyle. This has been on the books for years. Vivian got the resort in Vail. Meredith will get the one in San Diego when she's twenty-five. Coleman, if he ever gets his head out of his ass, will get the one in Vancouver, but I'm not holding my breath on that one."

"What about Natasha?" Mentioning the youngest of their siblings made him smile. The kid was pure sunshine and constant energy.

"Your grandfather didn't assign a property for her since

he made the will when all of you were little. She came along after and he never got around to it. But she's graduating in May. I'm sure we can find a place for her." Another long drag.

"Send her to Texas, Mom."

"Oh, sweetie, that's a lot for her to do straight out of college. She'd need a lot of guidance. You're ready to walk right in. Besides, *you'd* get far more hotel traffic than she will."

"You mean morbid curiosity." Nausea slammed him in the gut. The last thing he wanted or needed was to be gawked at by people who simply wanted to see the result of a huge Hollywood scandal. "I'm good where I am right now."

"Why? No one knows who you are." Her words were laced with annoyance.

"They know I'm a fireman and a paramedic."

"As if that's who you really are."

"I like the anonymity." *Although I don't know how much longer that's going to last.*

He tapped his finger on the envelope that held his proofs for the Men of Marietta calendar. Even he had to admit, the photos Charlie had taken were impressive and the calendar would cause all sorts of buzz. *I hope the right kind of buzz, because Harry deserves a place worthy of his name.*

Despite her promise to keep him out of any social media blasts and the *Vanity Fair* interview, he didn't trust his secret would stay that way for long. Especially with his mom breathing down his neck to fulfill his family obligations.

"You act like you're ashamed of us. You know, we're not just *anyone* in Hollywood. Our family's been in the business since there was one here. Patrick was a third-generation set designer and I've produced a lot of movies." She sighed. "Not to mention the hotels your great-grandfather started."

"I get it. We've got money. Influence." Kyle imagined his mother's nose stuck so high in the air right now, if it rained, she'd drown. "I'm not ashamed. I want something different. Something outside the bubble."

"The bubble is a damned nice place and has given a lot of good people solid work and very nice benefits. I want to continue that."

"I agree." His teeth ground together. He didn't need her guilt right now. Not when he had a nice evening already planned out with his gorgeous new neighbor. "If I want to spend it fighting fires and hauling people out of danger in Montana, that's my choice."

"I'm tired of having this kind of conversation with you. You've already played soldier, now firefighter. By your thirty-fifth birthday, you promised to fulfill this request of the will. If you don't, you forfeit your inheritance."

The thought of running the Jewel of the Hill Country no longer spread excitement through his veins like it did when his grandfather asked him a decade ago, but he wasn't stupid. That kind of inheritance would open a lot of doors for him and any family he might have.

That kind of money and influence had the potential to

help the people who needed a place like Harry's House.

Annoyance simmered in his gut at wanting a life here and to fulfill his obligation there.

"Mom, my birthday isn't until October. We've got some time to figure this out."

"You're stalling."

"Yes, I am."

"Why? A life in a town of maybe twelve thousand can't be that exciting."

"It's exciting enough for me." *And away from the paparazzi's constant coverage.*

Glancing out his kitchen window at his new neighbor's house, he smirked. *I hope it's about to get more exciting.*

"I can give you another few days, but I can't stall any longer."

He rubbed the back of his neck as he watched the seconds tick away. *Five minutes.* "Why?"

"Because I know something's off down there…*Junior.*"

Kyle's blood pressure shot into the stratosphere at her successful attempt to goad him. "Don't call me that. You know damned well that's not my name."

"Legally—"

"Goodbye, Mother—"

"Wait! Wait! I'm sorry." Another long drag, before she responded with about as much compassion as a crocodile. "Look, *Kyle*. I need you there. I'm pretty sure that general manager, Riley Fitz-what's-his-name is tanking my favorite resort."

"It's Fitzgerald." *And I don't like him, either.* The times Kyle had cold-called the resort for different questions and concerns, the manager had been this side of shitty. "Why do you think things are off?"

"A friend of a friend called because her brother's daughter got married there. The bride kept getting doused with a wayward sprinkler near the reception. Riley refused to take care of it or even compensate for anything."

Kyle cringed. "What a piss-poor thing for him to do. He should know how batshit crazy people get about weddings. That, at the least, was crap for customer service much less the bride getting wet at her own reception. What happened?" Not that he really wanted to know, but simply asking instead of attempting to talk his way out of this conversation would get it done quicker.

"They called in some local who fixed it right up, but the damage had been done. Now this bride is posting it all over social media about how terrible the resort is."

"He's Preston's friend. Did you expect anything less?"

A long pause. "I know you're mad at me for bringing Preston into the fold and then employing his friend Riley, but I'm trying to extend a hand to your father's side—"

"That man is not my father." *Four minutes.*

"Look, whether you like it or not, Jason Crowe is your father and that makes Preston Crowe your brother."

"Only genetically." He knew her forehead would be

completely scrunched up out of frustration if she hadn't let her dermatologist inject a gallon of Botox in it.

"Kyle, I'm sorry. I know you don't want the press to know anything about you after what I and your fath…Jason dragged you through, but you have to take care of this. It's your obligation. Your grandfather would be heartbroken if this property failed."

She always knew how to pull on his heartstrings when it came to family, but the calm of Marietta had sunk into his soul. Brought him a peace he'd desperately needed. Shoving the guilt away, he replied, "Mom, I have to go do something tonight, but let me talk to you in a few days about it."

"How many is a few?"

"A few." He checked for his keys again and started turning off lights. His boot caught on the edge of one of the donation boxes. Some of the coats scattered across the floor. "I left that world for a reason. Don't drag me back into it."

"Kyle—"

"No, Mother. Just give me a few days."

A long pause. "Even if there was someone on the inside of the resort, an employee who could tell you what's going on, it would help us figure out what the next step should be."

He slid on his coat and zipped it up. "Maybe you should send one of your attorneys down there, see if they can find someone."

"I could, but I have no idea who to trust when they get

down there. To whom do they talk?" she whined.

"I don't know, Mom. Even if I left right now and drove down there, how would I know any better?"

"That's a fair thing to say."

His finger hovered over the red button to end the call, but she didn't say anything. He wondered if she was still on the line. "Mother?"

"Did you see the magazine?" she growled.

Here we go. "Thanks for sending that, Mom. For rubbing my nose in it again."

"You know I don't blame you for him being your dad."

You damned well better not. "Glad to hear it."

"The affair was my fault. Our fault. All of us, but I don't want you to be anything like him."

"Mom, I know who I am and it sure as hell isn't Jason Crowe."

She sniffed mournfully. "I miss Patrick."

"I know you do, Mom. I miss Dad, too, but it's been ten years."

"I didn't mean to hurt him; I really didn't."

Good Lord. She does this every stinkin' time she's not getting what she wants. "Mom, it's history. I've got to go."

"Please, Kyle."

"Mom, I can't talk about this right now. I'll call you soon." He hung up before she had a chance to inject the right amount of guilt to get him to crumble.

As he walked next door, he allowed the crisp air to cool

down his anger. He got out of all that celebrity crazy for a reason. Here, no one looked at him with pity or around him to see if his famous parents were close by.

Here, no one had their hands out or wanted something from him.

Here, he could simply be a former vet and first responder and help people who truly needed it.

Yet, the desire to fulfill the promise he'd made to his grandfather burned in his gut.

Dammit. I can't have both.

A hard gust of frigid wind whipped around him, shaking his angst loose for a moment and helping his brain refocus on the evening at hand.

Gabriella.

In the illuminated room upstairs the shadow of someone walked back and forth across the window.

Wonder if that's Gabriella's room. He stood in front of her house like John Cusack in *Say Anything*, except he didn't have a boom box.

His heart raced as his breath came out in quick puffs of white vapor.

Why this particular evening had him so tightly wound, he had no real idea. For the first time in a long time, he wanted to make a good impression when it came to a woman.

Breathe, Cavasos. Just breathe.

Chapter Five

AT EXACTLY SEVEN, with his gifts in hand, Kyle knocked on their door once before it flew open.

"Cat Man! How's it hanging?" Trinity gave him a fist bump before she stepped aside. "Come on in. Gabby'll be down in a minute. She's fighting with her mother on the phone."

"Sounds familiar."

"Fight with your mom, do ya?"

More than I should. "From time to time." He stepped around the neatly stacked piles of boxes. "You got unpacked."

"We got the trailer and car unpacked. Tomorrow, we'll start getting this stuff where it needs to go. I'm guessing it won't take long. Helped that they had the big stuff here for us to use." Her eyes went wide. "Did you bring us groceries?"

He held up the bags.

She pointed to the kitchen. "You know where it is."

He liked this kid. She had a confidence about her that most girls her age didn't, but having Gabriella as her mother, he didn't find it at all surprising.

While he unloaded the cooler bag, she pulled the other items out and set them out on the table. "Dude, Oreos! Doritos. Dog food. Cat food. You rock."

"Figured you didn't have time to get to the store today." In their refrigerator sat a couple of individual yogurts, a small apple, three cheese sticks, and a half-eaten pint of blueberries. In a small, clear box remained one square of chocolate topped with a decent layer of what looked like powdered sugar. "Looks like you needed some help here."

"This is a great start."

Large flowerpots sat in the corner. Those same plants sat in his grandmother's kitchen. Cilantro. Bay leaves. Cumin. Poblano and serrano peppers. "I didn't know what fruit and vegetables you needed or if anyone was allergic. I see the plants made it okay."

"No allergies here. With Gabby being a chef, we eat just about everything."

He unpacked the refrigerated items as Trinity spread out the other contents on the kitchen table. A flash of red caught his attention. A small bunch of dried ancho peppers hung next to the pantry.

Delicious flashbacks of his grandmother's kitchen played through his mind as Trinity continued.

"We weren't sure what would be available up here herb wise, especially with the longer winters, so she brought her own." The teen ran her long fingers through her dark hair before pulling it back into a loose ponytail. "Besides, you can't make good *Pico de Gallo* without cilantro and some good serranos."

His mouth watered at the mention of the familiar herb. "It's been years since I've had good *Pico*."

"Impressed you know what it is."

"My grandmother used to make it all the time. She was a good woman. Great cook." *Funny how seeing something like plants could bring back such a sweet memory.* "You two get some sleep?"

"We crashed hard for most of the day. Only got up a few hours ago. Figured we could hit the grocery store after dinner."

"Monroe Grocery closes at eight."

Trinity's eyes went wide as she checked her watch. "Seriously? Why?"

"Small town. They roll up the streets early here."

"That'll take some getting used to. Lone Star Crossing's close enough to San Antonio, even if the local stuff wasn't open, we didn't have to drive far for what we needed 24-7."

"Texas? That's a long way from here." *Lone Star Crossing? Why do I know that town?*

He folded up the cooler bag and tucked it in an empty drawer. "How long were you driving?"

"What's today? Wednesday? We left Sunday."

"Damn, that's a lot of driving."

"Pulling the trailer and bringing the animals, Gabby wanted to give us enough time to get here. She officially starts at the diner on Monday, but I'm sure she'll drag me up there before then."

Belle wandered in and shook her tail when Trinity poured her some dog food in a bowl that sat near the back door. The old dog plopped down and pushed the nuggets around with her nose.

"How is Belle liking the snow?"

The corner of Trinity's mouth twitched. "Not sure. She's seemed to think it was okay, but she only ventured out about five feet outside the back door."

"Something I forgot to tell you, make sure to dry her paws when she comes in from the cold."

"Really? Why?"

"They can get frostbite between the pads of their feet."

"Oh, wow. I'll make sure we do that because we want to keep our sweet Belle safe. Isn't that right, puppy?" Belle closed her eyes in bliss and groaned as Trinity scratched her back.

"How old is she?" Kyle leaned against the counter, admiring the teen's kindness.

"We guess close to twelve or thirteen. Gabby found her eating out of the dumpster behind the resort where she worked. Brought her home and has taken care of her ever since. She has a thing for strays." The confidence in Trinity's eyes waned for a moment before she yanked opened the cookie bag and removed two Oreos. She paused. "Ever had a *Brownie Picante*?"

Her abrupt change of subject made the corner of his mouth twitch up. "Can't say that I have."

She grabbed the lone chocolate square out of the refrigerator and handed it to Kyle. "Try it."

Although Kyle wasn't into sweets, he accepted the gesture without question. "Thanks."

"Come. Sit. Gabby will be down in a minute."

"Thanks. What is it?" The red streaks through the powdered sugar worried him.

"A spicy brownie."

"What's the spice?"

"Crushed ancho pepper."

Holy shit! "Aren't those hot?"

"Only if you use too much." She motioned him to eat it. "Don't tell Gabby I said this, but hers are the absolute best ones on the planet. She's a magician when it comes to balancing flavors."

The small bite of chocolate didn't appear to be anything amazing, but he'd had experience with anchos that had cleared his sinuses. "What's in it?"

"Quit being a wuss and eat it."

Kyle smirked at her directness. As soon as the treat touched his tongue, Kyle thought he'd gone to heaven. The moist brownie gently rested on his palate as the combination of the chocolate, butter, and cinnamon layered perfectly while the subtle bite of the ancho pepper blended with the powdered sugar.

She'd created a perfect, decadent moment in a dessert that had every nerve ending of his body buzzing.

An instant addiction developed.

He licked his lips after finishing the last of it. "Got any more of those?"

"Good, huh?" She smirked and motioned for him to follow her to the living room.

The remaining sweet sat in his mouth and offered a temporary distraction to what the house looked like when the heat was up and the lights were on.

Depressingly brown.

The couch, chairs, throw rug, curtains, and walls were all some uncomplimentary shade of tan.

Even the cheap paintings and fake flowers had very little color.

Anyone who walked in here would get instant seasonal depression.

At least they had a big picture window in the front, which would allow plenty of natural light in, but right now, the heavy brown curtains were drawn.

Thankfully, the brownie's burn lingering on his tongue helped lift his spirits. "I don't think I've ever been in this house. It's, um—"

"Totally dreary." Trinity rolled her eyes. "I mean seriously. It's like they shopped at the burlap bag store. It sucks the life out of you as soon as you walk in."

"That's one way to put it."

"I mean between Gabby and I, there's already enough brown in his place."

The teen's honesty made him laugh out loud. "Brown is a good color."

"Depends on the brown. Like Gabby and I are more like melted milk chocolate with whipped cream mixed in brown. Totes fab." She patted the wall behind her before plopping down on the very boring couch. "The paint color on the cans I found in the garage, the swatch said, Drab Brown. Can you believe that? Drab. Brown."

"Sounds like the paint-naming guy sucked at his job." He took a seat across from her in one of the well-worn khaki-colored La-Z-boys.

"Indeed." Quick footsteps on the stairs alerted them to Gabriella's arrival. "Getting the ten-cent tour, I see."

He rose to his feet. "Yes, Trinity said she planned to color up the place."

"She's always got great ideas." She motioned for him to sit and she took the chair next to him.

"You want to tell him what you wanted to do?"

Trinity's eyes lit up. "I'll use some of my big canvases, paint them, and we'll clean things up, get some of our stuff out and it'll look, like, one thousand times *mucho* improved."

Nodding at her enthusiasm, Kyle asked, "You're a painter?"

"Paint. Sketch. Draw. Design, not that I expect I'll get

much of that at the high school here."

"I hear the art teacher is pretty good. She might surprise you."

She gave him a sad smile. "I like that you're positive. Gabby needs that."

Gabriella squeaked, but kept her composure. "Thank you, Trinity. Positive people are always a good thing."

"How do you know or care about art?"

"My younger sister, Meredith, paints." His response flowed out of him without pause. He mentally kicked himself since he hadn't planned say anything about his siblings.

"Oh, where is she?" Resting her elbows on her knees, Gabriella leaned toward him.

"Lives in Southern California." He about bit his tongue in half to keep himself from saying anything else. The last thing he wanted to do was give any inkling of who his family members were, especially with the press already buzzing about Meredith's art show in the next couple of weeks.

"California, huh? Good for her. A lot of artists out there."

"A lot of people who think they are artists out there."

The teen's smile morphed into a curious smirk. "That's what I hear, not that I've even been out there. Gabby and I have only lived in Texas. Barely been outside of the state otherwise."

"Not been outside of Texas? Why?"

Laughing, Gabriella asked, "You been to Texas?"

"A time or two." *Like when my dad helped build the set for Jason Crowe's popular sci-fi flick* His Alien Bride—*and to visit my grandparents' hotels.*

"It's a big place. Lots of things to do there and places to go."

"Plus *Abuela* likes to keep her kids close by." Trinity smoothed out her already smooth pants. "I love her, but man she can be smothering."

"Moms can do that," he chuckled.

"Yes, they can."

Kyle enjoyed her snarky humor. Trinity reminded him of himself at that age. Full of hope and frustration. Not knowing that life was about to hand you a bag of crazy you had no idea existed. His phone buzzed again. He ignored it.

Standing, Trinity excused herself for a moment and disappeared down the hall.

As soon as her daughter was out of earshot, Gabriella explained, "My mom, *Abuela,* just misses us, that's all."

"I have no doubt. Texas is a long way away."

Standing, Gabriella rolled her shoulders and then her head from side to side. "Sorry. It was a long trip. My shoulders are all out of sorts."

"I bet." His mouth went dry as she moved. *I can think of a good way to work out the kinks.*

Her dark hair cascaded about her shoulders. She wore jeans and a dark blue, long-sleeved T-shirt that fit her like a glove.

He took note of how perfectly the fabric hugged her curves. He never thought he'd be more jealous of a shirt than he was right now. Suddenly, his jeans felt uncomfortable. He shifted his weight to subtly adjust himself. *Get your mind out of the gutter.* Refocusing on the dull colors in the room brought his simmering libido down to controllable levels. "Moving to Marietta. A big change like this must be difficult for both of you." *I know my big change came out of nowhere.*

"Not really. We were both ready for something different." Clearing her throat, Gabriella nodded. "It's not every day that we get the chance to go on such an amazing adventure. Isn't that right, T?"

"Sure." Her less than enthusiastic response dulled the conversation for a moment as she entered with her phone in her hand. Her fingers sailing across the screen. "How far is Bozeman again, Kyle? That's where the closest art store is."

"If the roads are clear, you can make it in about thirty to forty-five minutes." An unexpected push on his leg made him look down. Cookie the cat rubbed up against him, spreading her white fur all over his carefully chosen outfit.

"That won't be bad. Maybe we can head over tomorrow," Gabriella added with all the happiness of a stressed Disney princess.

"If the roads are clear. Otherwise, I'd suggest you wait until you're comfortable driving in this weather." He reached down and pet the cat. "Or I could drive you."

"How chivalrous." Trinity scooped up her messenger bag and the most recent issue of *US Weekly* fell out. "Kind of like a knight in shining...you know, you should pose for me sometime."

"What?"

"Trinity Elise!" her mother shrieked.

Holding her hands up in surrender, Trinity cringed. "Sorry, my brain tends to jump from idea to idea like frogs on hot rocks so hear me out."

Kyle's heart slammed into his ribs as the teen stared at the magazine cover then at him a few times. Stuffing his hands in his pockets in an attempt to look casual, he shrugged. "What is it, T?"

"You've totally got a movie star jawline." She tiled her head as her eyes narrowed and her finger tapped the cover. "Anyone ever tell you, you look like this actor, what's his name..."

Don't say it. Don't say it.

She snapped her fingers as her eyes went wide. "Jason Crowe?"

"From time to time." His knee nervously bounced at a rapid tempo.

"It just occurred to me, you seriously look like him."

Since he hadn't read the article, he had no idea if any photos of him or his siblings were on any of the pages. His heart pounded so fast, it hurt. Casually, he lifted a shoulder despite his impending panic. "Jason Crowe, huh? Sorry kid, not the best compliment. That guy's a jerk."

Trinity nodded and tossed the tabloid on the coffee table. "You're right. He can't keep it in his pants for five seconds. Kind of like Gabby's ex-boyfriend, Derrick."

Again, Gabriella squeaked at her daughter's commentary. "And now you know my dating history. The end."

He couldn't help but laugh. "Fair enough."

Cookie jumped on the armrest next to Kyle. He scratched the cat behind the ears and she purred loudly before she settled into his lap. He appreciated the cat's approving purr even as his angst bubbled below the surface.

Trinity pointed. "You know, that's totally cool Cookie likes you."

"You mentioned she didn't like many people." A large pile of snow-white cat hair quickly accumulated on his jeans. That—along with the spilled powdered sugar from the brownie—made him look far less presentable than he'd hoped to be this evening.

So much for great first impressions.

"She sure didn't like Derrick. She peed in his shoes a bunch of times." She mumbled the last of those words before looking toward the front window. "That's one of the reasons we're up here. To get away from him and, you know, some other stuff."

Her wounded expression pulled on his heartstrings. He knew that look all too well. He saw it in the mirror every day when he thought of Jason Crowe and how he'd betrayed the man Kyle forever thought of as his father, Patrick Cavasos.

How could you have called him your best friend, Jason, then slept with my mother?

Kyle gently removed Cookie from his lap before standing and attempting to brush himself to be presentable.

"Okay, who's hungry?" Gabriella slapped her hands together.

The women grabbed their purses and sweaters before heading for the door.

Trinity zipped up a light jacket over her sweater and put on fingerless gloves.

He pointed. "You have heavier coats than that, right?"

They shook their heads.

"You can't go out without a heavy jacket. You'll freeze to death."

"How cold is it?" Gabriella asked.

"In the twenties."

"Good Lord! And I'm guessing nothing is open right now where we can buy coats?"

"They roll up the streets early here." Trinity rolled her eyes as she plopped on the couch. "Guess we're staying in. Who delivers?"

Kyle chuckled. "Nobody."

Slamming her hands on the couch, Trinity screeched, "Oh, my gosh! Where did you move us, Gabby?"

Tears welled in Gabriella's whiskey-brown eyes. "Trinity, please. I'm doing the best I can."

Again. Great. Nothing like a teen tantrum to send a nice evening down the shitter.

"Look, we can bundle up in layers. It'll be fine."

Holding her arms out, Trinity scoffed, "I'm already wearing everything I can."

Gabriella sniffed, but when Trinity didn't move off the couch, Gabriella gave Kyle a stressed smile. "I'm so sorry. It looks like we may have to take a rain check. Seems we didn't really prepare for the weather."

"It was in the seventies when we left home," Trinity snapped. "And now we live in Antarctica."

"Antarctica is in the Southern Hemisphere," Kyle replied before remembering the boxes in his living room. "Wait here."

Within a few minutes, he'd returned with a couple of thick coats, gloves, and hats.

Relief flooded across Gabriella's face as she donned the red turtleneck sweater and put on a thick blue coat. "Burberry? Where did you get these?"

Dammit. In his haste to secure their date, he'd forgotten they were high-end clothes. "People are donating to the new kids' center. People always need extra clothes in all sizes."

Kyle had to bite his tongue as she pulled the thick fabric over her body. The rich scarlet only accentuated her natural beauty, making her more breathtakingly gorgeous.

"Looks good," he squeaked and cleared his throat. "Seems to fit." *Better than any woman should wear a sweater.*

Trinity zipped up a thick, bright pink ski jacket and slid on the matching hat with the multicolored pom resting on the end. "Wow. Kate Spade."

Shit. If that doesn't make them ask questions, I don't know what will. "Glad they fit."

"Oh, you know, this reminds me of that movie that Jason Crowe was in."

The mention of that man slapped him harder than the winter winds that had kicked him in the face when he walked outside moments ago. "What?"

"Movie star Jason was some secret king or rich guy or something or other and gets the girl a coat because she's time traveled from some place. Apparently, they only wear tiny bikinis in her world. She was really cold wherever his kingdom was. Kind of like that chick on the cover of *US Weekly*."

Sounds like Jason's kind of movie. He plastered on his best smile as angst churned in his stomach. "Haven't seen it."

"Just as well, sounds ridiculous. I've never liked that actor. A man who'll cheat on his family like that isn't a man at all."

Great, she knows my story. "Agreed."

Gabriella pulled the jacket's collar close to her face and blissfully sighed. "It's warm. I've been fighting to get warmed up all day."

Despite her harsh words about his father, Kyle swallowed hard as his mind raced with plenty of ways he could keep her warm. "Looks great on you."

"You sure you're not a secret prince or billionaire or related to that movie star guy?" Trinity asked as they walked down the front steps, the pom on the top of her beanie winter hat bouncing with each step. "Because you sure look like you could be."

"Not a prince that I know of." Kyle laughed through his worry about the teen figuring out who he was.

And if she does, that would ruin everything I've worked for.

Chapter Six

THE RICH FLAVORS of chicken tortilla soup and grilled cheese sandwiches hit Gabriella's nose as soon as they entered the diner. Every muscle in her body relaxed as she soaked in the ambiance.

Mine. The word coursed through her veins as Kyle escorted them to a table nearer to the kitchen and away from the door's intermittent cold.

My diner. My business.

Being from a large family, she had always struggled for her own share of anything from clothes to food to the twin bed instead of having to sleep next to one of her sisters or cousins in the full-sized ones. Even though it was over a thousand miles away from home, knowing this place had only her name on it gave her a feeling of pride she couldn't begin to describe.

Booths lined a wall as tables filled in the rest of the room. Red leather-covered, short-backed stools sat in front of a long counter. The seats were solidly grounded into the wooden floor but appeared to swivel with ease. The large kitchen pass-through window was big enough to get a quick view of how far back the kitchen stretched and to the left, a set of three-quarter, wooden swinging doors led to the back.

The solid redbrick wall opposite the front door begged to be painted. Although a sturdy structure that separated the diner from the business next door, Gabriella could imagine some amazing mural, something eye-catching as customers walked in.

She suppressed her excitement as her tired brain revved up with ideas, but her cheeks hurt from smiling so hard as she took in every inch of her new adventure.

Even through the thick sweater and coat, she could feel Kyle's gentle hand as it rested on her shoulder. He pulled her chair out, a chivalrous gesture. "For you."

"Thank you." *A guy who knows manners. His mama raised him right.*

As soon as Trinity plopped her messenger bag and her heavy coat in the spare chair, Kyle held a seat out for her before she could claim her own. He flashed her a winning smile. "Young lady."

"Thanks." She gave him a smile, but when her eyes met Gabriella's, angst washed over them. "I don't see any kids here my age."

"Calm down, sweetie. It's going to be okay."

"Hey, Flo." Kyle hugged the woman who gave him a quick kiss on the cheek as he settled in.

"Visitors?" She pointed with the pencil she'd grabbed from behind her ear.

"Flo, this is Trinity and Gabriella Marcos. They just arrived this afternoon. Moved in next door to me."

The woman's thin eyebrow cocked up. "You wouldn't happen to be the Gabriella who now owns this place, would you?"

She hadn't expected such a rushed introduction, but Gabriella nodded and extended her hand. "Yes, that would be me. Nice to meet you, Flo. Paige has told me so much about you."

The waitress enthusiastically responded in kind. "We don't have too many Gabriellas pass through here, much less move into town."

"Oh?"

"And Paige sent your info and photo. Said you had rented the house next to Kyle." The corner of her pink-lined lips curled up as she filled their water glasses. "Welcome, but I have to say, that picture didn't do you justice, sweetheart. If we weren't busy before, we're gonna be swamped when word gets out that you're here all the time."

"No kidding." Kyle sucked his bottom lip like the words had unintentionally jumped out of his mouth.

The heat of embarrassment swept across Gabriella's face. "Thank you both."

Her daughter looked over each of her shoulders. "I don't see any other kids my age here."

Reaching out, Gabriella patted the table in front of her daughter. "It's Wednesday night, honey. They are probably at home. Please, it's going to be okay."

Flo set the water pitcher down and pulled a pencil from behind her ear. "What can I get for y'all tonight? We've got chicken tortilla soup, apple-cinnamon pork chops and of course, this guy's favorite, pot roast."

"That's why you suggested we come here. Got a soft spot for stick-to-your-ribs type of food." Although Gabriella had no idea how Kyle could have a body that looked like his and eat such rich food. She'd only seen him in his loose workout clothes and now cleaned up. It didn't matter he had on layers of shirts or a heavy coat. The thickness of his arms and the broadness of his shoulders made it quite obvious that the guy had abs you could bounce quarters off of.

And I've got three rolls of quarters.

A mischievous grin spread across Kyle's face. "You got me. Always loved it, since I was a kid. Never make it for myself though. Takes too much time."

"You could always use a crock pot." Gabriella shrugged. "Not much effort. Just need to add the spices, throw in some beef broth and let it cook for six to eight hours. It should fall apart."

"That's true." Flo nodded as a few more customers came in. "But you'd have to convince this guy to use something other than lemon pepper if he makes it himself."

"I bet I could show him all sorts of ways to spice things up." The words registered after they spilled out of her mouth and Kyle raised an eyebrow.

"I mean, I could teach him about different spices."

Trinity stifled a giggle.

That's a mental headslap for sure.

"I'd appreciate learning how to spice things up." Kyle gave her a quick wink that just about melted her panties off.

Fanning herself, Flo waved to another person who sat down at a table with four other men. "Evening, Carson. The usual to start?"

"Much obliged, Flo." He tipped his hat before removing it and sitting at the table.

Knowing the established customers only added to the excitement of the night. Gabriella's heartbeat kicked in a notch. "Regulars, I'd guess?"

Leaning toward Gabriella, Flo whispered, "Those are the Scott brothers. Here every Wednesday. There's five of them."

Gabriella craned her neck to get a better view of the group as they sat close to the window. "Is that their regular table?"

"No, they pretty much take where they can sit. Annie's the wife of Carson, that big fella that I said hi to. Annie works here a couple of times a month, but not on the nights Carson comes in with his brothers."

"Is there a reason for that?"

"Sure, she's having girls' night with the Scott wives." With her pencil, Flo pointed to different people around the room. "That's Casey. She's a full-timer."

A short, dark-haired girl with a nose stud gave them a nod as she picked up an armful of plates from the kitchen pass-through window and headed over to the Scott brothers' table.

"Four plates at a time. Impressive." Gabriella smiled.

"Casey's brother, Brett, works with Kyle." Flo playfully patted Kyle's shoulder, but his jaw clenched.

What's that about? "The cook's name is...?"

"Merlin. He and his brother, Griffin, trade shifts. Both have worked here for years. We had Mrs. Thorpe here for twenty years, but she retired awhile back when the diabetes made it hard for her to work."

"Is that Colton's mom?" Kyle asked.

"Yes. The very same. We've got a third cook works weekends. Travis. He's a senior in high school."

Despite Paige sending all this information to her, Gabriella appreciated putting names with faces. "Thank you for the introductions, Flo. I'm looking forward to getting to know everyone on Monday."

"Monday, huh? Not tomorrow?"

The question unexpectedly unnerved Gabriella. "Monday was when I planned to meet everyone. I wanted to give myself a day or two to unpack. Get settled in."

Flo made a clicking noise with her tongue. "That is a long drive, I hear. Rest up. I'm pretty sure I can hold down the fort until Monday."

"Thank you."

"Okay, Kyle. Pot roast with double mashed potatoes or were you needin' a side of broccoli this time?"

The countertop bell rang as Merlin yelled, "Order up!"

"I'll take both, Flo." Kyle patted his stomach. "And a slice of the lemon pie if you've got any."

"I'll save the last slice for you, but that's a lot of food. What's the occasion?"

"Working at Harry's House tomorrow. Reconstruction day."

"That's right. You boys will be working on getting the place up to code. And here I thought you were stocking up to work at the station." She playfully slapped his arm.

It suddenly occurred to Gabriella she knew very little about her neighbor. "What kind of station? Radio? TV?"

"Fire."

Well, that just sent him up about fifty points on my sexy scale. "I didn't realize that."

Flo patted Kyle on the shoulder. "Marietta's finest first responder."

A fireman? Another fifty points. Gabriella wanted to sit on her hands to keep from fanning herself. "Good to know."

"He's *one* of the first responders, not the only first responder," Casey murmured as she ran by with a tea pitcher in each hand.

Apparently, Kyle didn't hear the waitress's comment, because as Flo continued to brag about him, a slight blush colored his cheeks. His obvious embarrassment didn't appear to slow down her compliments. "How long have you been living here, Kyle?"

"Close to a year."

"We're glad to have you." She tilted her chin up and then turned to Gabriella. "What can I get for you, boss?"

Gabriella liked the sound of that. "Me? Whatever you think is good, I'll try."

The sizzle of something being tossed on the grill danced though the half-full dining room right before the thick flavor of perfectly seasoned beef, with a hint of onion, followed.

Her stomach growled. Eating on the road had thrown off her body clock and she couldn't remember the last good meal she'd had.

Flo gave her a nod. "Fair enough. And you, Trinity? What can I get for you, darlin'?"

The teen shrugged, her elegant fingers playing with her new hat. "Not sure."

"We can make just about anything. Chicken. Beef. Pork chops. Sandwiches. Soup. Salads."

"I wish they had *barbacoa*." Her eyes glistened with unshed tears. "I would really love some."

Oh goodness. Her favorite comfort food. For the past few weeks, Gabriella had made buckets of it. "T, I can make that this weekend if you want, but right now, Flo needs your order."

"No, no, we've got barbecue. What did you want that on?"

"Sorry Flo. She said *barbacoa*." Kyle answered before Gabriella had a chance.

"Not sure what you're sayin' then."

"It's like pot roast. Served in a gravy. Made from the head and cheek meat of cows."

Holy crap! He knew what barbacoa *was?* Kyle shot up her sexy scale so fast, Gabriella was pretty sure she'd be pregnant by dessert.

Even Trinity looked impressed.

Flo continued to stand wide-eyed. "What?"

"It's served at a lot of Mexican food places."

"Are you serious?"

Impressed that Kyle even knew how to say Trinity's favorite dish much less what it was made of, Gabriella added, "It's good. The meat is really tender, but the traditional way is to cook the entire head in a pit, in the ground."

Scratching her head with the end of her pencil, Flo shrugged. "I'm not gonna have anything close to that."

"No problem, Flo." Turning to her daughter, Gabriella reined in the angst that slammed around her gut like trapped hummingbirds. "What do you think, sweetie? Pot roast? I see they have grilled cheese."

The fear in her daughter's eyes broke Gabriella's heart.

Flo walked around and rested her hand on Trinity's shoulder. "Darlin', Merlin makes an incredible grilled cheese. Will put any kind of cheese you want on it. A lot of the kids around here love it. Isn't that right, Frederick?"

A young man's voice answered, "Sure is, Miss Flo."

"Frederick goes to the high school." She nudged Trinity. "What grade are you in, again, sweetie?"

"Freshman."

"Frederick's a sophomore." Flo's tilted her head over Trinity's left shoulder. "Frederick picks up dinner for his parents every Wednesday. Don't you, Freddie?"

"Sure do, Miss Flo."

Flo excused herself to check another table.

The teen spun around in her chair as Gabriella cocked her head to the side.

The young man walked over to the table from the counter, his eyes only on Trinity. "Hi, I'm Frederick. Call me Freddie."

Her daughter chewed on her bottom lip for a second before answering, "I'm Trinity. Call me, um, Trinity."

Kyle gently elbowed Gabriella and gave her a wink.

Excitement bubbled in her gut as she watched her daughter twist a lock of her hair between her fingers while she spoke to the young man.

Oh, my goodness that's adorable. But within seconds of considering the situation endearing, a mama-bear fierceness slapped her from out of nowhere.

Oh, Lord. What if she wants to start dating?

As if he could read her mind, Kyle rested his hand on hers and gave it a gentle squeeze. "Don't worry."

"This is my…Gabby." Trinity randomly pointed without taking her eyes off her new friend.

Standing, Gabriella extended her hand. "Nice to meet you, Freddie."

He responded in kind. "Ma'am."

"Freddie." Kyle stood up and Freddie flinched, but shook his hand as well.

"Sir."

They all stood in awkward silence for a moment before Flo arrived.

"Here you go, Freddie." Flo handed him a takeout bag. "Tell your mom we all said hello. Stay warm."

"Thank you, Miss Flo." He gave them all a respectful nod. "See you soon, Trinity."

"Bye, Freddie," they all answered, and Trinity giggled once the young man was out the door.

They all settled back in their chairs.

In an attempt to avoid embarrassing her daughter, Gabriella didn't say a word about what had just happened, but she couldn't be more thankful for the warm welcome by the locals. "T, what did you want for dinner, sweetie?"

A dreamy look settled on her daughter's beautiful face. "Did Flo say they had good grilled cheese sandwiches?"

"Two roasts and a deluxe grilled cheese, Merlin." Flo yelled as she walked by their table before attending to new customers who'd walked in.

Immediately, Trinity pulled out her sketch pad and feverishly began drawing.

A calm nestled in Gabriella's heart as she watched her daughter's eyes sparkle while she made the pencil sail across the paper.

Well, that's a good sign. She's drawing again. With the chaos of the last few weeks, her daughter hadn't created anything new.

"Trinity told me you drove for four days to get here?" Kyle leaned forward as if he were about to tell the most interesting story. "What part of Texas did you drive from again?"

"Near San Antonio, a town called Lone Star Crossing."

"I don't *think* I've ever heard of it."

"Don't worry. Most people just say they're from San Antonio. It's an easier landmark."

He flashed her a playful smile. "Fair enough."

Gabriella wrung her hands in her lap to keep them from reaching out and feeling just how thick Kyle's biceps were. "I wanted to give us plenty of time. Pulling the trailer and having the animals certainly proposed some challenges, but—"

"But we had to stop in Fort Collins to visit my aunt," Trinity interrupted, a slight pout on her face as her pencil froze just above the pad.

"It was a nice visit, Trinity. We hadn't seen her for years. She's been overseas."

"She's in the military?" Kyle took a drink of his water.

"No, she works with Hewlett-Packard. She's been in Ireland, but after twelve years, she decided now would be a great time to come back to the States with *her* daughter." Trinity eyes glistened with unshed tears and it broke Gabriella's heart.

Why couldn't her family have been kinder and less obvious of their disapproval? As usual, Gabriella tried to put a positive spin on a shitty situation. "Yes, so you have a new cousin."

"Does your sister like Fort Collins?" Kyle removed his wool-lined jacket and set it on the back of the chair.

The curve of his shoulders that fed into his arms made Gabriella's mind wander to naughty thoughts...until she realized he'd asked her a question. "It's not my sister. It's Trinity's mother's sister who lives there now."

His forehead furrowed. "*Trinity's* aunt then?"

"Exactly. With her having moved back to the States, we couldn't pass up an opportunity to see her. Right?" Smiling, Gabriella hoped Trinity would smile back. Instead, the teen didn't respond, but had returned to focusing on her creation.

Turning her attention back to their dinner companion, Gabriella clasped her hands in her lap. "A fireman, huh? That's cool."

Well, that was an eloquent segue. Gabriella mentally cringed.

"And paramedic. Been here close to a year." Kyle nodded as his eyes darted back and forth between the women as though he were trying to figure out their story.

Don't even try, buddy. Your head will explode at the drama.

"What made you want to be a fireman?"

He lifted a shoulder. "I'd already been a corpsman. Seemed like a good transition."

"I don't recall Flo mentioning you were a veteran. What branch?"

"I was a Marine Corps Force Recon, so a Navy corpsman."

Good grief. I don't think I can take him adding any more sexy to his résumé. Gabriella shifted in her chair, trying to quell that flutter between her legs. "A Marine Corps Force Recon. That's a mouthful."

"Say that five times fast." He chuckled before taking a drink of his water.

"San Antonio has quite a few military bases."

"I did my medical training there. More than half of all military medical personnel train in San Antonio."

Now his knowledge of Mexican cuisine made sense. "Is that why you knew what *barbacoa* was?"

"I ate a lot of Tex-Mex while stationed there." He patted his stomach. "Had to run many miles on the Riverwalk and the missions to burn off those meals."

She appreciated his self-deprecating humor and the way the edges of his eyes crinkled up when he laughed.

And the width of his shoulders.

And what he probably looked like naked. *Please don't have said that out loud.* "Adrenaline junkie, huh?"

Another round of flavors drifted through the air. This

round had a hint of seasoned salt, but smelled heavy on the pepper.

"More like a helping people junkie, although it seems that helping people does require a certain amount of risk taking."

"Anyone else in your family—"

"Nope. I'm the only one who's a first responder." He shifted to his left. "What are you drawing, Trinity?"

His sudden shift in conversation made her head spin. *Guess his family isn't his favorite subject.* "Trinity has won several awards for her artwork. She's quite talented."

"I do okay." She pulled her precious sketch pad close to her body as though she didn't want him to touch it.

He encouragingly tapped the book with his index finger. "Can I see?"

The teen looked at him like he'd grown an extra arm out of his forehead. "Why?"

"Why not? If you've won awards, I bet whatever you're drawing is great."

The frustration on Trinity's face began to wane as her shoulders relaxed. "Seriously?"

He patted the table. "Come on. I can only draw stick figures and even those suck."

Good to know he's bad at something. Although drawing would be one of the last things on her mind if Gabriella ever did get a date with this guy.

It took about three seconds before Kyle's chipper mood

became contagious. The corners of her daughter's mouth curled up as she flipped through her sketches, explaining each one.

As the two talked art, Gabriella looked over the menu. The battered plastic-sleeved pages were a good sign of a busy restaurant, but the subtle wear and tear signified the need of a little TLC.

The metal, cushioned chair she sat in wobbled slightly, as did the table. Some of her daily maintenance would be spent completing basic repairs since a place this busy was in constant need of a tweak here and there.

Good thing Mom and Dad taught me how to fix things.

Trinity's laughter pulled her away from ideas about the diner. How she loved hearing her daughter's joy. *There hadn't been enough of it lately.*

Scanning the room and seeing what people ate, Gabriella noticed the same kinds of dishes seen in so many small-town diners.

I could expand the menu a little, maybe specials for Sunday or weekends? I wonder what they'd say to themed food days? Seasons? Use what local farmers grow.

"What do you think?" Flo came up with a basket of bread and slid it on the table, pushing Gabriella's water glass a few inches over. "You thinking of changing much?"

She refolded the menu and placed it back in the holder. "Just looking over things. Getting an idea of it all."

One of Flo's over-plucked eyebrows arched. "Paige told me about the cooking school you went to."

"The Culinary Institute gave me a great education. I loved it." As accommodating as the woman had been, Gabriella could tell she was worried about her job security. Gabriella knew exactly what to say to calm the loyal employee's angst. Resting her hand on Flo's arm, she encouragingly replied, "But I have to say, nothing can be as good as cooking with moms and grandmas and longtime friends. They add something to a kitchen that you can't get out of a book or a class."

"Amen to that." Her dangling monkeys-holding-bananas earrings gently swayed. "Looking forward to seeing what you bring to Marietta."

"Thank you, Flo. I appreciate that more than you know." *Especially after what happened at the Winston.*

A bell rang from the kitchen. "Order up!"

In less than a minute, Flo returned with their plates. "Two pot roasts, one with double mashed potatoes, and a deluxe grilled cheese. Oh, I'll get your broccoli, Kyle, and I didn't ask you what you wanted with your sandwich, Trinity."

"Can I have fries?"

"You got it."

"Thanks, Flo."

The heaping helping of pot roast and the two mountains of mashed potatoes took up the entire eleven-inch plate set in front of Kyle.

Gabriella smirked at the feast, but Kyle had to be well

over six feet and having the kinds of muscles she imagined, a man would need his protein sources. "You're really going to eat all that?"

"Yep." He broke off a large chuck of meat and attacked it like a T-Rex, giving her a wink as he devoured it.

Oh, what I wouldn't give for you to devour me like that.

Her eyes went wide at her erotic thoughts.

Thank goodness I didn't blurt that out. What in the hell is wrong with me?

She nibbled on the pot roast as she tried to sort out why her libido had gone on overdrive since this morning.

You're exhausted.

You're overwhelmed.

You haven't had sex for over a year.

"What do you think? Good, huh?" Kyle asked, his green eyes the color of new grass in springtime.

Yeah, it probably has to do with the guy sitting next to you. "Yes, it's very good."

Watching Flo work, Gabriella noticed how easily the woman glided from table to table. She seemed to know almost everyone and what customers liked and didn't like. She was for sure an asset and someone Gabriella didn't want to lose.

Gosh, I hope she stays. Being in the restaurant business for close to a decade, Gabriella knew a new owner could certainly make established staff as skittish as newborn colts. *Hopefully, I can win their trust quickly.*

As they ate the perfectly cooked pot roast, Gabriella and

Kyle discovered each of them were movie lovers and read voraciously.

"How many brothers and sisters do you have, Gabriella?" Kyle asked as he used the last piece of his roast to soak up the gravy.

"Eight. I'm in the middle of nine." The remaining hints of garlic and beef from the perfectly tender dish still sat on her tongue. Regretfully, she washed them down with the rest of her water.

"That's a busy house."

"Not all are your actual siblings—right, Gabby?" Trinity interjected after having remained silent for a while. "A couple are cousins. *Friends*."

The strain on the word friends pulled on Gabriella's heartstrings. "That's true, Trinity. But we all grew up together. We help each other. Support each other no matter what."

"Sounds like family to me." Kyle shrugged before finishing his drink. "Some of the best people I'd call family were friends."

Trinity pulled her last sandwich triangles apart. A long string of cheese dangled between them before she bit it in half. "This is the best grilled cheese I've ever had."

"See, I told you." Flo refilled their water glasses and removed completed plates. "Coffee anyone?"

Gabriella nodded. "I'd love a cup."

Kyle held up two fingers while Trinity happily ate the

remaining French fries.

"I'll bring it with the pie." Within a minute, Flo returned with two steaming mugs of coffee, a cup of individual creamers, forks for all, and one huge slice of lemon meringue pie.

A perfectly browned crust cradled the bright, gooey yellow filling and was topped with a two-inch thick meringue.

"Thanks, Flo." Kyle gave her a wink.

"It's something we've had on the menu for years." The waitress looked at Gabriella with wide-eyed angst. "It's a popular item."

"Then I can't wait to try it." Plastering on her best smile, Gabriella grabbed a fork. As the tongs plunged into the pie, the crust's flaky layers gently fell apart. "Oh, my goodness. I can already tell this is going to be magnificent."

Flo's eyebrows hit her hairline. "You can?"

"The crust came apart perfectly."

"You hear that, Casey? The crust is perfect."

Casey gave a less than enthusiastic thumbs-up.

The tart of the pie hit Gabriella's tongue about two seconds before the sweet of the meringue, layering exquisitely. She couldn't help but close her eyes and bliss out on the dessert. "Wow."

Flo's excitement only increased. "That good, huh?"

"That's amazing."

"Told you it was good." Kyle helped himself to another forkful.

"Wouldn't change anything, then?"

Gabriella stopped the words before she let them escape and lied, "Nope. Not a thing."

Giving them a wide smile, Flo nodded. "Well, looking forward to working with you, boss."

Boss. Gabriella really liked the sound of that.

Chapter Seven

THAT WENT BETTER than I thought it would.

Kyle had forgotten the pressure of wanting to impress someone, especially over a meal as messy as pot roast and mashed potatoes. At least he hadn't dripped any on his clothes.

But the best part of the night had been when Flo introduced Trinity to Frederick.

He hadn't forgotten the awkwardness of teen years. He well remembered how hard it had been to meet good people, especially after his family's scandals wouldn't quit making headlines.

Washing his hands, he gave himself a mental pat on the back for how well the teens' introductions had gone.

After meeting the ladies this morning, he'd gone by the diner and asked Flo if anyone Trinity's age came in during the dinner rush. Thankfully, Frederick Westbrook always picked up dinner for his mom, Shelly, on Wednesdays when she'd work a double at the hospital.

Flo knew when he'd usually arrive and said she'd give an easy, non-pressured introduction. As always, Flo kept to her word.

Seeing the general new-kid-in-town angst disappear from Trinity's face had been a complete one-eighty since she'd muttered the words, "I don't see any kids my age."

Then the fantastic the sparkle in Gabriella's eyes of seeing her daughter make a new friend made the stealth worth it.

Of course, it had been funny watching that happiness morph into protective fierceness on realizing her daughter had made a new *male* friend.

It was all Kyle could do not to laugh out loud and it only made him like his new neighbor even more.

Glad to know she takes the job of motherhood seriously.

As he exited the bathroom and popped a mint, he noticed Gabriella talking to a few of the locals. Her dark hair rested gently about her shoulders and her kindness radiated into the room as if being in this diner was the most natural place for her to be.

He leaned against the doorframe and simply watched her for a moment. For obvious reasons, he'd always found beautiful women intriguing. Female company, he'd never been short of, but many of the starlets he'd met over the years were as vapid as they were gorgeous.

Not Gabriella. She'd already shown herself to be smart, beautiful, and quick-witted. Without even trying, she'd kick-started his repressed lust that he'd tamped down since he arrived in town. Being in the same room with her had him so tightly wound, he worried he'd bust his zipper.

Thank God for thick coats.

His phone buzzed and he glanced at it. His mother had texted him again, this time with a link to reviews of the resort.

Dammit, Mom.

The melody of Gabriella's laugh tickled his ears. *I can't leave now. Not yet.*

He turned off his phone as his mind continued to search for some loophole in all this.

They'd said their goodbyes to the diner staff and headed out into the frigid night air.

"Ready?" He rubbed his hands together before he opened the door, preparing himself for the frigid air that slapped him in the face as soon as he walked outside.

Quickly, they made the short distance to his car and buckled up.

"Holy crap! It's cold." Trinity's teeth chattered. She pulled the cap over her ears.

He turned up the heat. "I'd usually make this a walking tour but considering the windchill factor is in the teens—"

"Are you kidding me?" Trinity dramatically pulled the collar of her jacket to her nose as she complained. "How cold does it get here anyway?"

"In the dead of winter, a lot colder than this."

Trinity mumbled something about living at the North Pole. "Should I expect elves or a guy in a red coat walking by?" Frustration laced her commentary.

"No, we give the big guy off the month of March. Won't see those guys around until at least September." Out of the corner of his eye, he watched Gabriella bite her lip.

A giggle came from the back seat. "Okay, okay. Well played."

With a stressed smile, Gabriella added, "Thank you, Kyle. That was incredibly nice of you to take us to dinner."

"Glad Flo took the sale well. Sometimes, people don't respond well to outsiders." Not that he could complain much. The townsfolk had taken him under their wing almost as soon as he arrived. He had Harry to thank for that.

"She was lovely. It's comforting really. I see it in her eyes."

"What's that?"

"Seeing she loves the diner and cares about what happens to it. Those kind of employees are hard to come by."

Her sincere positivity warmed his heart. Without realizing it, she'd shown herself to be a polar opposite from the dripping sarcasm he'd grown up with. "That's one way to look at it and you're right. Flo's been at the diner for a long time."

"I hope she and I can work well together for the benefit of the place. The only thing harder than finding dedicated employees is finding supervisors who appreciate and respect them." She gritted her teeth at those last few words. After running her fingers through her dark hair, Gabriella shook her head. "Sorry, my former boss was…difficult to work with."

"He was a thieving ass," Trinity mumbled before shaking her head in frustration. "And his daughter was…was…"

"We don't have to deal with either one of them anymore."

Is that why you're in Marietta? As much as he wanted to ask, he wouldn't. At least not tonight. Slapping his hands together, Kyle stated, "Ready?"

"For what?"

"Said I'd give you a tour."

Reaching across the seat, Gabriella gave his hand a quick squeeze. "That would be lovely."

"I don't mean to be snarky, but I'm guessing this isn't going to be a long tour." With a shrug, Trinity pulled out her phone. "I mean the town isn't all that big."

"You never know, Trinity. Sometimes looks can be deceiving. Small towns can have a lot of unexpected, wonderful treasures," Gabriella said.

It took a moment for Kyle to process Gabriella had been staring at him when she'd complimented the town.

Her dark eyes sparkled as the corner of her mouth slightly curled up.

At that moment, he thanked his lucky stars his coat covered his lap. The instant hard-on she gave him with that sweet smile of hers made him adjust in his seat before shifting the car into drive. "Well said."

With it being a Wednesday night and after eight, along with the frigid temperatures, most of downtown's businesses were closed with the exception of Grey's Saloon. The lighted beer signs flashed at them as he slowed at the intersection. "That's Grey's. It's been here since the town was founded in the 1880s. Ephraim Grey opened it and the family has run it ever since."

In the backseat, he saw Trinity's eyebrows rise. She glanced out the window and looked up. "Is there an upstairs?"

"Yep. It's got a pool table and bar up there. A staging area for special events."

"Eighteen-eighties, huh? A lot of history. Bet that building would say a lot if it could talk."

Considering it was a bordello at one time, I'd bet it would have plenty to say.

Kyle tucked that comment away. He had no idea how knowledgeable Trinity was about the facts of life. Putting Gabriella in the weird situation of having to explain anything had to be one of the last things he wanted to do tonight.

Not great first date protocol.

He pointed buildings out as they drove, popping back a couple of peppermints he kept in his cup holder. "That's the Western wear store. You can get some nice clothes in there."

Gabriella nodded. "Not too far from the diner."

"My friend Harry—" The man's name came out like glass against his throat. He cleared it. "Harry's sister, Joanie, runs it. You might want to ask her about some heavier clothes."

"Oh, you think we'll need more than what you gave us?"

He chuckled. "It's cold like this for another few weeks."

"Wow. This is a lot different from Texas." Trinity glanced out the windows. "It's bluebonnet season there now."

Remembering the fields of rich blue flowers that could be found all through the Texas Hill Country and beyond, Kyle nodded. "That's right. Blankets of them, if I recall."

"Yes."

"Ever drawn any, Trinity?"

"Oh, yes! I have some here in my book. I'll show them to you when we get back."

"Looking forward to it." As she shuffled through her drawings, he took his time driving, pointing out the businesses down Main Street that either of the women might find interesting. "There's the bookstore, Java Café, nail place, chocolate shop. Up here on the right are the school district offices, the elementary, junior high, and high schools."

Motioning toward the high school, Gabriella leaned forward. "There weren't too many cars in the parking lot this morning when we drove in."

He realized he hadn't let go of her hand and she hadn't pulled away. His heart rate jumped. "The high school starts after eight here because of the roads needing to be cleared in the winter. No point always having to call a delayed school start."

"So you get to sleep in a bit." Gabriella looked over her shoulder at her daughter. When Gabriella moved, the subtle floral scent of her hair floated in the air and tickled his nose.

He inhaled and blissed out on the fragrance.

"Well, that's one good thing." The teen nodded.

Stopping at Fifth and Main, Kyle asked, "You're in high school, right, Trinity?"

A reluctant nod from the back seat. "I'm a freshman."

Gabriella cleared her throat. "Trinity's birthday is in the summer, so it looks like she's a year younger than a lot of her peers, but she's in all Pre-AP classes."

"An artist and a scholar, huh?" Kyle glanced in his rearview mirror. "Good for you."

As they passed one of the streetlights, he noticed Trinity's grin from his compliment. *At least she had a good sense of humor.* "I can hear the school bells go off from the fire station."

"Eight will come early, especially when it's this cold."

Kiddo, you have no idea what it's like in the dead of winter. Saving those tips for another conversation, he pointed. "The gas station, and here we have fire and police stations."

A sudden giggle escaped his front-seat passenger. "Sorry, you're a fireman, right?"

"Yes, and a paramedic."

Gabriella shifted in her seat. "How interesting."

"Something like that. There's Tyler Carter's gym across

the street where a lot of us work out."

Gabriella craned her neck. "Police station next door."

"Speaking of art, can I buy art supplies anywhere around here?" Trinity's fingers drummed on the door handle.

"To the left here, Big Z's hardware store will have some of your stuff. Basics, but for the canvases and specific brushes, you'd have to order online or drive to Bozeman."

"There's Big Z's coming up on the left." During their slow tour, Kyle pointed out the Chinese food place, the movie theater, pizza parlor, and the Graff Hotel.

"That's the Graff, huh?" Gabriella leaned close enough to the passenger window that Kyle could see her quick puffs of breath on the glass. "Paige showed me pictures. She said it had a major overhaul. Supposed to be beautiful inside."

"Maybe I could take you there, sometime." *Dammit, Cavasos. Quit being weird. You don't pressure a woman you've got trapped in your car for another date.*

"I would like that." A gentle squeeze from her hand sent shockwaves through his body.

Maybe it's not so weird.

Carefully, he turned onto Court Street as a gust of wind whipped between the buildings, shaking the car. "This storm is going to be ugly."

"Is it supposed to snow?" The girl's eyes were wide with anticipation. "I mean, I know it's ridiculously cold and all, but I've never seen snow fall before."

"Looks like someone's adding powdered sugar to everything." Without thinking, he turned on Church and slowed before turning at the intersection of Church and Second.

Trinity's head popped out from the oversized coat collar like a turtle does from its shell. She looked out the opposite window and pointed. "What's Harry's House?"

Swallowing hard, Kyle lingered at the stop sign. The makeshift, windbeaten poster board sign sat on a stake at the bottom of the steps. The streetlight's glow was just enough to see it at night. "It's going to be a center for kids. Serve breakfast, after-school snacks; there'll be classes, study groups."

"They didn't have anything like that back home. I just hung out in my grandmother's salon after school a lot of the time."

The subtle excitement in the teen's voice brought a smile to Kyle's face.

With no one else around, Kyle backed up and easily parallel parked in front of the building. "Wanna go in?"

The two women couldn't unbuckle their seats fast enough.

Once inside, Kyle flipped on a few lights. "These are the original hardwoods."

"It's beautiful." Gabriella gasped. "Mind if I look around? I won't touch anything."

"Sure." The faint smell of dust lingered in the crisp air.

Slowly, she wandered through the rooms with child-like wonder. "This is going to be amazing."

"The kids in town need a place, especially during the winter." He followed her, intrigued by her interest in an old, remodeled house.

Trinity tapped the doorframe with her knuckles. "More drab brown paint. They must have had a sale."

"That's gonna change. If you want to see the colors we're using, I've got the paint colors upstairs."

"Thanks, I'll go check in a minute. Gonna go look at the kitchen."

Multiple ladders, sheets of new drywall, buckets of paint and plaster, as well as a large Igloo cylinder water cooler lined the far wall. The windows were delivered yesterday and he'd already separated them into groups for each section of the house.

The increased pounding of his heart echoed in his ears as the joy of anticipation built in his chest. He couldn't wait to get started on the next phase of the project. Kyle always felt better after he'd fixed something. "You can't really see it all that well, but the outside trim is green. They've painted it already, but I think it needs an extra coat. Inside, it needs a lot of work to get it functional."

"What do you have to do to get it to code?" As she ran her hands along the walls, Gabriella's footsteps echoed through the house. "Are you just getting started or finishing…? Oh, just getting started."

It took him a second to realize she'd asked and answered the question. "How would you know that?"

She tapped the bucket of plaster with her boot. "The seal on those buckets of plaster aren't broken. You've got no trash anywhere. The new windows are still wrapped. Some of those tools look like they've never been used."

Damn, this woman knows about home repair, too? Would there be anything he wouldn't like about her?

"You know a thing or two about construction?" The subtle floral scent of her hair tickled his nose and caressed his face as they walked into one of the back rooms. With Trinity out of sight, Kyle counted to ten to keep himself distracted enough to not lean in and start nibbling on Gabriella's perfect earlobe. He swallowed hard when he ran out of numbers.

Be a gentleman. Be a gentleman.

She opened a closet, glanced in, and closed it. "My family knows a thing or two about getting things put together."

"There are two things you learn about being in Gabby's family." Trinity had wandered in.

Kyle looked over his shoulder. "What two things?"

"You learn how to fix things and you learn how to cook."

"Speaking of cooking, how did you know about *barbacoa*?"

The amusement in the teen's voice brought a smile to Kyle's face. *Score one for me.* "Other than being stationed in San Antonio?"

"Yes."

"My grandmother used to make it."

Gabriella's eyebrow cocked up. "What's your last name, again?"

"Cavasos."

"Cavasos." A slow smirk spread across her face. "Your father's mother or mother's?"

"Father's." His maternal grandmother was a loving woman, but she had plenty of help. *She probably didn't even know where the kitchen in her house was.*

"You learn to cook too?"

"Nope, I can make one thing. Lemon chicken."

"It's better than macaroni and cheese," Gabriella gave him a wink. "Sounds like you got more on-the-job training about fixing things than cooking."

"Something like that." *Too bad I'm about the only one out of my siblings who learned.*

Trinity approached the wall behind them and swept her hand over it like she held a large paintbrush. "What does *Abuela* say, Gabby?"

Without pause, the dark-haired beauty replied, "*Vengo de una familia muy chambeadora, sin miedo al trabajo.*"

Hearing the familiar words float over her full lips just about set his pants on fire. "Which means…" he managed to squeak out.

"Basically, we're a hardworking family."

"Does your mother have any other sayings?" It wasn't until that moment he realized how much he missed hearing the easy tempo of the language his father spoke to him on many occasions. *Please talk more Spanish to me.*

She faced him. "Sure. *Mi abuela era una extraordinaria cocinera y mi abuelo no había nada que no supiera arreglar.*"

He watched her lips move as she spoke, loving the way the double *R*s rolled off her tongue. The way the sounds flowed together like melted chocolate.

When her eyes met his, Kyle worried if he got any more turned on, he might bust his zipper. "Translation, please."

A healthy blush colored her cheeks as the gentle scent of whatever perfume she wore danced around him. Gabriella's eyes zeroed in on his mouth. "It means—"

"That my grandmother is a great cook and my grandfather can fix anything." Trinity stepped back still facing the wall as though she were eyeing a canvas.

Nothing like a teen stepping in to kill the mood.

"Thank you, Trinity." *Well, that worked better than a bucket of ice water poured down the front of my pants.* Kyle mentally laughed off his libido.

"You're welcome. I'm gonna go look around some more." She peeled off her coat and hat, tossing them to Gabriella without asking before leaving the room. "This is very exciting."

His father's side spoke Spanish growing up, but since Patrick's death, Kyle hadn't kept it up. Now, learning that Gabriella spoke it, he seriously considered digging out that unopened Rosetta Stone language program sitting on his shelf upstairs.

In the meantime, he'd keep asking her questions because the more he learned, the more his addiction for her grew. "Does Trinity speak Spanish, too?"

Adjusting the extra coat and hat in her arms, Gabriella nodded. "She speaks some. I think she can understand it more than she speaks it, but she would do fine in a class at school."

"She's a smart kid."

Gabriella blew out a long breath, kind of like his mom used to do when he'd pushed her to the edge. "She's a great kid. What's the budget for this place? Was it bad?"

"Not terrible, but we're hoping the money we're raising helps cover all the costs plus some operating expenses."

She sighed contentedly as she ran a hand along the original wood doorframe, as if this were the most comfortable place for her to be. "Really, what are y'all doing to raise money?"

His lust continued to climb as he watched her lovingly trace a line of imperfection in the wood. He had to unzip his coat to make sure he didn't burst into flames. "There was a bake sale."

She smirked. "Really? How did that go?"

"Decent. They raised over thirty thousand. Covered all the inside remodel." He motioned toward the hallway. "Show you some more of the place?"

Her eyebrows hit her hairline. "Good grief, thirty thousand? That's a lot of cupcakes."

"The guys made it and they auctioned off what was made."

"Ah, yes, hot guys and cookies. Always a winning combination. What did *you* make?"

Her compliment took him off guard. "I didn't make anything. They didn't ask."

"Seriously?"

Placing his hand in the small of her back, he walked her into the back room. The large window looked out into the darkened backyard. "Speaking of making things, we're going to make all this a kitchen back here, extend it from in there. Easier access for cooking classes. More natural light."

He patted the wall behind them.

She peeked around the corner and cringed. "Those '70s cabinets should be the first to go. They don't match the tiled countertops at all."

Narrowing her gaze, she pursed her lips as though deep in thought. She stood in the doorway between the two rooms. "Knocking out part of this wall out will certainly help open the place up. Since it's load bearing, you can't knock it all out, but you can certainly remove this middle section. Make an arched opening."

"Why arched?" His heart raced in anticipation of her answer.

"Because the arch is the strongest structure you can have in a building."

"Right." If her daughter weren't here, he would have

kissed Gabriella until they were both naked and screaming each other's names. She might be under layers of clothes, but Kyle had a pretty good idea how beautiful her curves were.

Clueless to his growing libido, she pointed. "Might want to consider an island where the kids can sit around it, hang out. Good place to do arts and crafts. Cooking classes."

"Not a bad idea." *I'm gonna have to sit in a snowbank by the end of tonight to get my sheets to lay flat.*

"Nice that the appliances are all on one side of the kitchen in there. You don't have to run new lines to everything. What do you mean they didn't ask you to bake anything?"

It took him a second to realize she'd returned to the Bachelor Bake-Off. "Didn't ask me? The Bake-Off? They only needed a few guys."

"They raised enough money, then?"

He didn't like where this conversation was headed, but he couldn't lie. She'd find out about the calendar shoot sooner or later. "No. Afterward, we found out there were some foundation issues. Underground water. Drainage problems with the house."

"Yikes, that puts a heavy price tag on it. What are y'all gonna do?" She cringed as she opened and closed the cabinets. "You know, these might just need to be stripped and new handles put on. Might save a few thousand."

"I think that's what we decided to do, but to answer your question, we had to come up with some other ideas. Something different. Hopefully, it'll work. Out back, there will be a large garden."

"A garden sounds nice. Anything I can do to help?" Closing the gap between them, she took his hand. "With the fundraising, I mean."

His mouth went dry at her touch. Clearing his throat, he replied, "No, no, it's all taken care of. Charlotte took care of it."

"Charlotte?"

"Charlotte Foster. Charlie. The photographer. I think she might be seeing Logan Tate right now. He's a deputy sheriff."

"Photographer? What did she come up with?" Her eyes sparkled with excitement. "You think this new fundraising will be enough?"

"I sure hope so." Kyle had already decided if their project didn't raise enough, he'd make sure Harry's House received an *anonymous* donation to carry them not only through the repairs but a couple of years of operating costs as well.

Of course, he should have done that before Charlie sweet-talked them all into posing. Then he wouldn't be so damned worried about the stinking thing going viral and Jason Crowe hearing about it.

I wouldn't put it past him to attach his name to anything that would make him look human, especially after the last tabloid headline he caused.

Kyle knew it would be great numbers for Harry's House if the actor mentioned it, even once, but it would blow

Kyle's chances for any kind of normal life here in Marietta and he'd be forced to move on sooner than he wanted to.

She rested her hand on his cheek. "Hey, you okay?"

The warmth of her touch made his body tingle. "I'm good."

More than good.

"You sure? I'd be glad to help with whatever you need. Donate supplies or help with cooking."

"Thank you, Gabriella, but this isn't anything you use in the kitchen."

"Oh. What's the fundraiser, then?"

Damn. He did not want to talk about this. "I guess you could hang it on the wall."

Her eyes went wide. "On the wall? Like a poster?"

Stuffing his hands in his jacket pockets, embarrassment washed over him. "More like a calendar."

"You posed for a calendar?"

He swallowed hard at the lust that washed across her face. "It's for a good cause."

"I'm sure it is. What month are you?"

Chapter Eight

WHAT MONTH ARE you?
Good grief, Gabby, could you say anything more fangirl?

Still, the idea of this guy standing in whatever means of undress, hanging on her wall year-round, made the move to Marietta instantly worth it.

"Oh, um, I'm October." His bright red cheeks only made him all the more adorable and sexy.

Oh, so sexy.

Her eyes betrayed her, raking over him. "Mr. October. Well, that's a great month."

"My dad's and my birthdays are that month." Lust lingered in his eyes.

She rested her hand on his chest, unable to stop herself from wanting to be near him. "October is full of amazing things. Pumpkins. Apple cider. Hayrides. Football. Spurs basketball."

The beating of his heart hummed under her palm. When she realized how close she'd moved, she began to step away, but he rested his hand over hers. The soft gesture encouraged her to remain in place. "Glad you like October."

Swallowing hard, she stared at his lips. "Is the, um, calendar out yet?" *I'll buy a thousand copies.*

"Not yet. They're talking about having some sort of launch party in a couple weeks."

"How did the pictures, um, turn out?" *I'll buy two thousand copies.*

"Pretty good. I have the proofs at home." He leaned forward, his lips inches from hers. "Would you like to go with me?"

"To the calendar, reveal?" Peppermint laced his breath.

"Yes."

"Sure." *Hell, yes, I would.*

"Thanks."

Oh, no. Thank you. Tilting her head up, she inched her mouth closer to his before…

"You said I can check out upstairs—right, Kyle?" Trinity shouted.

"Yes, please do." Gabriella didn't move but noticed Trinity peek around the corner and gave a thumbs-up before her quick footsteps made the stairs creak.

"It's safe up there." Kyle rested his hand on the small of her back, gently encouraging her closer. "They're setting it up to be a study hall."

"Thank you."

"You're welcome."

She tilted her chin up, looking deep into his eyes. "Now,

where were we?"

He brushed his lips against hers, making a sigh escape her. "Somewhere about here."

"Yes." Pressing his mouth to hers, he slid his tongue along the seam. Her mouth opened and his tongue swept in. The burn of peppermint tingled along the sensitive skin and sent a thrill straight to her panties. She couldn't help but moan, which only appeared to encourage him.

He pulled her flush as he nibbled her lower lip.

Sliding her hands around his body, she heard a soft thud, but she didn't bother to look at what she'd dropped.

Her tongue slid along his, deepening their kiss.

He tasted of lemon pie and mint. It had been too long since she'd been engulfed in this kind of passion.

All consuming. Wild. Hungry.

It took everything she had not to rip that jacket and shirt off him and run her hands down that chiseled body she knew he hid under his clothes.

"Gabriella," he whispered before nibbling on the pulse point of her neck.

She gasped, grabbing handfuls of his jacket. "Yes, Kyle."

"Damn, you smell good. Taste even better." His mouth covered hers again.

Even with Derrick, she hadn't experienced this kind of chemistry and certainly not this quickly. She ran her fingers through his hair as he moved his hands along the sides of her body. His thumbs tenderly brushed the outsides of her breasts. Despite the thick sweater, his touch penetrated the layers and set her body on fire.

"Gabriella," he gasped as he came up for air.

"Yes?" she panted, her hands running down his thick torso. Her fingers itching to move under his shirt.

"Would you like to go out with me?"

She couldn't help but giggle at his innocent question. "Are you asking me on a date?"

The corner of his mouth curled up as the flush of red on his cheeks began to fade. "Yes. I guess I am."

"Considering I just stuck my tongue down your throat, I'd say that's a yes on the date."

A lusty laugh escaped him. "Fair enough."

As heavy footsteps sounded on the stairs, Gabriella reluctantly pulled away and straightened her clothes. "Trinity's on her way."

He let out a long sigh. "Continue this later?"

"Yes." *Please, goodness, yes!* Tucking her hair behind her ear a few times in an attempt to look casual, Gabriella cleared her throat as the sting of peppermint still tingled on her tongue.

As her daughter neared the room, she spoke loudly. "Did I understand Flo to say you're working here tomorrow?"

"Yes, we're working all day tomorrow on it. Got a ninety-day deadline or the city takes it back." Kyle zipped up his jacket as he shifted his weight a few times.

"We?" She knew that shift. Good to know he was as

turned on as she was.

"The first responders. It's for a friend of ours. Harry."

The cross outside of town blipped in her mind. She could feel her forehead furrow. "Did he...?"

"Yes." Flashing a subdued smile, Kyle nodded. "Last Labor Day weekend. Hit and run."

"Oh, no. That's terrible."

"It's going to be a busy day. Lots of work to do."

Trinity appeared around the corner as Gabriella continued, "That's very interesting, Kyle. Thank you for showing me the house."

"Nice try, guys, but I know y'all were making out while I was upstairs." Trinity grabbed her jacket and hat off the floor. "The paint colors you picked out are going to be great. Let me know if you need help. I'll be in the car."

As frustrating as her daughter could be, Gabriella had to laugh at the teen's keen observation skills.

When they'd all settled back in the car, Trinity added, "Too bad Uncle Eddie isn't up here, Gabby. He and his friends would have that whipped up in no time."

"Yeah, he would."

Trinity settled back in the seat. "That upstairs area could be such a cool hangout like a media room—or I guess you could do a study hall type place with the media room downstairs. Be sure to put in a coffeepot or K-Cup machine."

"I think someone already thought of having upstairs as a

quiet room." Kyle turned on the car and cranked the heater, not that Gabriella needed it.

Her body still hummed from Kyle's touch—and the idea of going on a date with him. Her stomach felt like hummingbirds danced around inside. The delicious excitement of having a date with a hot fireman only verified her move to be the smart choice.

Not that you had many others.

He added, "There's also an attic. We'll need ideas for that. You want to help with some of the setup?"

"That would be cool. Don't you think so, Gabby?" Trinity asked.

The question pulled Gabriella out of her reverie. "What?"

"Don't you think it would be cool if I helped with the setup? Hey, maybe I could teach some art classes to the younger kids."

"I think that would be great." Getting a taste of Kyle only made her crave more. A whole lot more.

"What kind of work does your brother do?" Kyle turned down Second Avenue.

"What?" *Focus!* She had to yank her mind out of a lovely scenario of her unzipping his jeans, sliding them off his perfect ass, and seeing him in all his naked glory.

"Your brother? What does he fix?"

"Oh, Edwardo. Yes, he can fix just about anything. He knows how to work some magic when it comes to repairs."

She ran her fingers through her hair. "He keeps that resort up and running like a champ."

Kyle swallowed hard. "Resort?"

"Yes, where I used to work back in San Antonio. My brother is the head of maintenance there. That place would fall apart without him."

There was a giggle from the back seat before Trinity added, "Remember when he had to be called in about that wayward fountain hose that kept squirting the guests at that wedding?"

"That bride was pissed. Glad her pictures were done before she got soaked."

"Bride got soaked? How did he fix it?"

Did Kyle's voice just go up? Curiously, she watched him as she spoke. "He didn't at first. That jerk of a manager kept telling me he knew someone who could repair it instead of calling my brother in. He spent over a thousand dollars on a friend of his who said he was a plumber and then ended up almost ruining a wedding reception because of it."

"Your brother saved the wedding, then?" His hands gripped the steering wheel tighter than they had a minute ago.

"Yes." Gabriella shook her head as the memory of Riley Fitzgerald childishly stomping his feet replayed through her head. "Thank goodness we had the food protected in the tent, but that bride was not happy."

They pulled into the driveway and Kyle immediately put

the car in park. "What ended up happening?"

"As soon as the father of the bride threatened not to pay a dime for the entire event, they called Edwardo in on his day off. My brother fixed it within minutes. Just needed a couple of seals replaced and to adjust the hoses, all of which he had in stock. Of course, they didn't pay him any more for saving their asses. Not even a thank you."

"That's detrimental to the business if the manager's doing that kind of crap." Kyle's forehead furrowed for a moment. "It could ruin a place."

"That wasn't the first crap he'd tried to pull. You'd be amazed at the stuff that guy got away with."

"Did you ever talk to upper management?"

"No."

"Why not?"

Because he threatened to fire everyone in my family who worked there if I said a word. "I guess I didn't know if they'd believe me."

Gabriella glanced out the other window, not wanting her pent-up anger over Riley Fitzgerald to ruin her highly charged evening.

"But Uncle Eddie is awesome. I miss him," Trinity sighed.

"I'm sure he'd love to help if he were here."

With his jaw still clenched, Kyle nodded. "We could use all the help we can get. He sounds like a good guy."

"He's the best at his job for sure." Drumming her fingers on her leg, she pushed away the sadness of not seeing her oldest brother every day. "He's taught us a lot so if you need any help, let me know."

He popped his seat belt and clasped his hands in front of him. "Well, there's the tour. Any questions?"

"Thanks again, Kyle. I'll go check on the pets." Trinity gathered her bag. "I'm sure Belle needs to go outside."

"Don't forget to dry her paws if she's in the snow."

"Right." The back car door slammed. Trinity sprinted across the yard before Kyle had even closed his car door.

"Dry her paws?" Gabriella walked around to join him.

"Keeps Belle from getting frostbite between her toes." He held out his hand and she instantly grabbed it.

"Good to know."

Trinity ran up the steps, entered the house, and flipped the porch light on, leaving the door wide open as she called for the dog.

The winds whipped by Kyle and Gabriella as though they were shooing the couple across the icy grass to the warmth of her house.

Without thought, she grabbed his hand as they made quick work of the stairs.

She stopped short of the door and turned to him. "Thank you."

How she wanted to invite him inside, continue what they'd started at Harry's House, but she couldn't. Not with a huge lack of sleep and apparently no rational thought as far as he was concerned.

As if he could read her mind, he kissed her on the cheek.

"We're good, Gabriella. Get some sleep."

"Thank you so much for helping me, us, today." She shivered as a brisk wind whipped by them.

"Of course. Harry helped me when I first came to town. I'll help you."

"He sounds like a good guy."

Kyle grimaced as if he were in pain. "You would have liked him."

Stepping forward, she took his bare fingers, sandwiching them between her gloved ones. "I'm sorry to hear about your loss."

Kyle lifted a shoulder. "What can you do? It's done."

"It doesn't make it any easier." She began to ask him something, but a frigid gust swirled around them. A whimper escaped her.

"Go on. Get inside. We'll talk more tomorrow."

Relief flowed through her. She stood on her tiptoes and kissed him on the cheek before whispering in his ear, "Thank you, Kyle, for being such a gentleman."

"You're welcome, but I sure as hell don't want to be."

Oh, my! As she pulled back, her eyes focused on his lips.

Her body suddenly felt like she'd been thrown into a hot springs.

How she wanted to kiss him. Kiss him until he moaned her name deep into the night…but not tonight.

Tonight, as much as she hated the idea, she'd be her normal, responsible self.

Dammit.

Chapter Nine

During the short walk home, he hoped the frigid weather would be a good substitute for a cold shower, but no such luck. Like some wound-up teenage boy, Kyle resorted to the old-fashioned method of relieving his tension, but it only gave him temporary relief.

Not only did Gabriella have his dick in knots, but if what she'd told him about his grandfather's resort was true, he wouldn't be able to wait until his birthday to save it, either.

Clicking the link sent by his mother, he found multiple bad reviews of the management, but rave reviews about the food, salon, and general staff.

Running his fingers through his hair in frustration, the reality of leaving had been kicked up a notch.

He began to call his mother, but something made him stop.

I have to reread those papers again. I'm missing something.

By the time he got to page two, the legalese made him go cross-eyed. "What I need is a lawyer."

A name popped up in his mind and he quickly texted his

college friend, Dean Stafford.

When he didn't get an immediate response, he gave in to his exhausted body and overworked mind.

By the time he crawled into bed, he had trouble getting the sheets to lie flat or his mind to calm down considering he stared at the light from the upstairs window next door.

He wondered if she were still awake. If she were already in bed. If she slept naked.

How she'd feel next to him, under him, on top of him.

One thing at a time, Cavasos.

Sometime after midnight he drifted off, his thoughts on the woman next door and his approaching family commitment.

When the alarm beeped at five-thirty, he still tented his sheets as he held on to the last bit of a tremendously vivid dream of Gabriella and him and meticulously placed whipped cream.

Deciding the best course of action would be to run off his pent-up frustration, he hit the treadmill before a cold shower and a quick breakfast. He loaded up his truck with his father's toolbox in hand and three floor heaters, and drove the three blocks to Harry's House.

Being the first to arrive, he unloaded everything and set his precious toolbox on the counter in the kitchen.

Immediately, he walked through the building, making a mental list and writing jobs on the walls with his flat-edged pencil.

He placed the new windows near where they were needed to save time for the installers and to avoid confusion.

Standing on the second floor, he watched as the first light of the morning peeked over Copper Mountain.

Once again, Kyle marveled at the rich golds and reds as they poured over the white-capped peak. "Damn, that never gets old, does it, Dad?"

The frigid morning winds whispered against the single-paned windows.

The first time he'd watched the sunrise here happened back when his father brought him to Marietta on a long father-son ski weekend. They'd spent the entire time outside going up and down the slopes and taking in the local sights. Just them—a nice change from having to share his father's attention with four other siblings.

A nugget of pain pinched Kyle's chest at the memory of the multiple bruises his father sustained after those long days of easy skiing.

That trip was right before he got his first leukemia diagnosis.

Tears threatened to fall.

And the last time he looked at me without judgment.

Shaking off the grief, he shifted his focus to the knowledge his father had given him about home repairs instead of the sad memories.

Tears fix nothing.

As one of Hollywood's top set designers, Patrick Cavasos knew how to fix and create anything. Kyle had followed his father around from the time he could strap on a tool belt and absorbed every bit of information his dad shared.

Scanning the room, Kyle smirked. "Dad, you'd love fixing this place up. It's like that building you had to get ready for Mom's first movie and then the first one she directed."

The wind subtly tapped the glass as though it was answering him. He often wondered if his father spoke to him through projects like this.

When they'd picked this building for Harry's House, Kyle knew it would be a tremendous amount of work to get all the interior work completed. Still, he had full confidence he'd help everyone get the project done.

He had his father to thank for that. Without his dad's teachings, they'd all be wandering around this place, wondering what to do and making things worse.

The sun continued its rise, making the snow-capped peaks glisten as though someone had sprinkled gold flakes all over them.

He wondered if Gabby would be interested in such things. Sitting with him as he watched the sun come up each morning. Maybe they could watch through his upstairs window as they sat on the battered futon on the other side of the room from his treadmill.

The idea of holding her in his arms, the subtle fresh smell of whatever the hell that shampoo she used was tickling his nose caused his jeans to instantly become too small in the crotch.

Shaking off his infatuation, he needed to get his head on straight before the guys arrived.

The last thing they need is a foreman with his head in the clouds.

Once again, he walked the second floor, double-checking his to-do list and setting up the generators for heat; but he knew the Clark brothers would probably laugh at the heaters.

Being from Southern California, Kyle had taken a while to get used to the cold here. He'd come a long way this winter, but this morning had a chill about it he couldn't shake.

He had no doubt those guys would show up in T-shirts, jeans, and light jackets.

At exactly eight, a creak of the front door sent Kyle downstairs. "Mornin', Logan."

Deputy Logan Tate growled as he entered. "Let's get this done."

"Bad night?"

"Don't want to talk about it."

"Fair enough." Kyle couldn't help but smirk. Logan had been seeing a lot of photographer, Charlie, since she arrived in town.

The saucy Brit handled the photo shoots of the First Responder calendar like a pro, even allowing Kyle to partially hide his face. She didn't even ask him why and he respected her for that. But he guessed as professional as she was with the rest of them, Logan was another story. It wasn't a big secret that Logan and she had taken things into the personal arena. This had only been validated yesterday when their dispatcher, Betty, had whispered to Kyle that Charlie was seen buying a pregnancy test. "Charlie okay?"

"The woman makes me nuts," Logan mumbled as he put on safety goggles after checking his phone.

"Whatever's bugging you, work it out beating the shit out of something. You'll feel better." Kyle patted him on the back, handed him a hammer, and pointed him toward upstairs.

Without a word, Logan grabbed a mask and safety goggles, and followed Kyle, who instructed him on the most productive way to rip out the stud walls.

With Logan to work and others arriving, Kyle gave each man an assignment that he thought they could do with little or no supervision. Or at least without making things worse.

The Clark brothers—Jonah, Gavin, and Dan—arrived. They'd already offered to install the windows. He sent them up to start unwrapping them and getting them ready for install.

Forest ranger Todd Harris rolled in not long after that along with doctor Tom Reynolds.

Since these guys knew how to operate electric screwdrivers, he sent them into the kitchen to get all the cabinet fronts off, strip them of their hardware, and rip out the obnoxious blue-tiled countertops.

"Why do you get to be foreman, Cavasos?" snarked K9

officer Brett Adams before he tossed his to-go cup of coffee into the makeshift trash can near the front door.

"Because I know what I'm doing, Brett, and you're late."

"I had to walk the dog," he snapped as his faithful companion, Duke, sat patiently next to him.

Giving the dog a scratch behind the ears, Kyle added, "I can't have a dog on a job site, Brett. It's not safe for the dog."

"He can hang out near the door. I've got his blanket in the truck."

"No."

"Come on, man. I'm on call. Either I stay and help and the dog stays, or I have to go."

"Why can't your sister take care of him?"

"Casey's at work. At the diner."

Glancing down, the dog went doe-eyed as though to say, "Come on, man. Give me something. I want to help."

Noticing a corner away from the chill of the front door and close to a heater, Kyle relented. "Fine, if you've got his bed in the truck you can bring it in, but if he starts to wander or gets in anyone's way, you gotta take him home."

"Great." After setting up the dog's bed, water, and snacks, Brett returned for instructions. He grabbed a sledgehammer, but Kyle shook his head.

"Nope, we got enough of that demo going on."

"What am I supposed to do, Cavasos?"

"What can you do, Adams?"

"I can break stuff."

"Good, you can pull and install all the toilets on both floors."

Brett grimaced. "You suck."

"You know how to unscrew it from the floor?"

"It's not that hard."

"You know to make sure the water's off before you do?"

Brett's mouth went thin. "Yes."

I didn't think so. "Don't forget your safety goggles and mask."

"You still suck."

"Thanks for your help." With everyone working, Kyle made a sweep-through of the site and checked the dog before starting in on prepping to replace the fuse box.

For the next couple of hours, Kyle struggled to keep his mind on the task at hand. Only problem was: his new neighbor kept sneaking into his thoughts. If the fantasy of her slipping off her clothes and him finding heaven between her thighs didn't cloud his thoughts, the reality of his grandfather's resort would.

For now, the fantasy won.

After pinching his finger with wire cutters, he fought with the impossible task of getting Gabriella off his mind.

Why? He'd known her for barely a day and already the idea of being with her sat high on his to-do list.

Focus, Cavasos. Focus.

Yet, their kiss from last night still made his lips buzz.

Having her hands on his body gave him such rock-hard dreams, he wouldn't need a hammer to drive the nails into the wood.

Right in the middle of cleaning up his trash, his phone beeped. Greedily, he grabbed it, hoping Dean was returning his text, but disappointment slammed him in the gut.

Mother.

He growled as he shut off his phone. "Don't have time for this right now, Mom."

He tucked it in his back pocket, but after several more texts buzzed, he realized why Gabriella's smile had been such a powerful distraction.

Mentally scanning through the contracts that lay on his kitchen table, something tickled the back of his mind that might help him get both his life of anonymity and fulfill his family's obligation.

Or is that just wishful thinking?

When his mother texted him again, he left his phone on the downstairs windowsill to avoid hearing or feeling any more messages. "Watch my phone for me, Duke. You can eat it for all I care."

The dog wagged his tail and licked his lips.

Around eleven, an argument between Logan and his brother Lyle erupted from upstairs where Logan had been working since he arrived. After a few choice words and an apology, Logan handed off his work to his brother and stormed out.

By one, all the dead drywall, half the windows, and all the toilets had been pulled and thrown into the dumpster. They cleaned up the trash and swept before all decided to take breaks for lunch and come back in an hour.

Despite the midday sun, the temperatures sat in the thirties with a brisk windchill, but most of the men appeared unfazed by the weather as they dispersed in several directions to either head home or walk to a local eatery.

Frigid spring weather was simply a way of life here in Marietta, but a nice relief from the sweaty work they'd accomplished so far.

Brett decided to take Duke for a walk and let him run around Bramble Park, a couple of blocks away.

For whatever reason, Kyle simply didn't get along with the guy, but he did respect the fact Brett took his K9 officer duties seriously and treated the dog like family.

Walking the site again, Kyle heard the Clark brothers talking.

Reaching down, he scooped up several strips of molding and headed upstairs.

"What are you losers looking at?" Kyle asked as he entered the room, dropping the molding on the floor.

The three men were standing next to the window, looking out.

The two older, Gavin and Dan, were playfully elbowing the youngest, Jonah.

"Don't you have windows to put in? It's getting cold up

here." But Kyle knew these guys could easily stand in T-shirts and shorts when it snowed outside.

"You're right." Jonah angrily gnawed at his lunch. "But the two knuckleheads over there are busy people-watching."

Glancing out the window, Kyle saw a young woman crossing the street. He could only guess that the scowl on Jonah's face indicated the pilot didn't want to be asked anything about her.

But after an encouraging wink from Gavin, Kyle simply couldn't help but yank Jonah's chain. He quickly commented about her being too young for his tastes and her appealing look that screamed sexy girl scientist.

Jonah's face turned a bright shade of red.

Then Gavin and Dan explained who she was.

A nice girl. Knew her in school. Back in town after a decade away. Smart as a whip.

The more they talked about her, the more Jonah looked like he was one of those cartoon characters that literally blow their stacks.

Kyle smirked at the banter. He and his brother, Coleman, used to give each other grief this way. See how far they could push each other's buttons until one of them exploded or gave up.

Apparently, Jonah's limit was reached when Kyle asked if she was dating anyone. He lost his shit, demanding Kyle leave her alone.

"No worries, man." Kyle threw his hands up in surrender

as he moved away. Catching the smirks of Gavin and Dan, Kyle lifted a shoulder. "He's got it bad."

"Shut up, Cavasos."

For years, the longing for family had been filled with college friends, his time in the military, and now the first responders here, but it never quite filled that want to reconnect with his own family.

How he wished a single mistake hadn't sent the Cavasos family into total and unrecoverable chaos.

Shaking off his sadness, Kyle decided a quick trip to Big Z's hardware was in order. He needed a few more cases of caulk, as well as brooms, painter's tape, and garbage bags. Plus, he would check on the shipment of insulation that would be delivered within the week.

"How's the remodel coming along, Kyle?" Paul Zabrinski, owner of Big Z Hardware, asked as he rang up Kyle's order.

"Slowly. We're getting a lot done today, Paul. Add the insulation on this ticket, too, if you would."

"Um, sure. Let me know if you need any other help. I'm sure I can round up a few people."

Without thinking, Kyle swiped his credit card and signed for it. "I'll keep you posted. Thank you."

Paul's raised an eyebrow. "You're paying for this yourself?"

"Yep." Glancing at the wall clock, Kyle calculated how much time he had to get back and unload before the guys returned. "You have a good—"

"Don't you need a receipt?"

"No, thanks. It's fine."

"That's a mighty expensive bill there, son. You're not going to have the fundraising account cover it?"

The innocent comment froze Kyle in his tracks. Had he just paid for almost two thousand dollars worth of supplies without blinking an eye?

Dammit! "You're right. A receipt would be great."

You can't throw money around like this. People will start to suspect something.

"I wondered. Got your mind on other things I expect." Paul gently folded the receipt before handing it over. "We all appreciate you guys working so hard on that project. Harry was a good man."

"The best." He pushed the cart out as fast as he could go before he bought out the store. Kyle mentally kicked himself. He hadn't meant to use his credit card, but he'd been so distracted by his mother's calls and Gabriella's...well, Gabriella in general, that it didn't even compute he'd pulled out his wallet.

He chuckled at Paul's wide-eyed response when he said he didn't need a receipt. *If they only knew. My sisters have bought one pair of shoes that would make that bill look like penny change.*

As he unloaded the supplies into the back of his truck, high school history teacher Chelsea Collier walked by. She gave him a quick wave and he gave her a heads-up on the new teen in town and her mom. "She's a good kid. Into art and pretty sharp. She met Frederick Westbrook last night."

"That's a good start. He's a great student. Nice young man. I'd be glad to come by and meet her."

"Might want to start at the diner. Gabriella will probably be there too."

"Good idea. Kind of neutral territory." She pulled out her phone and her thumbs quickly tapped on the screen. "I'm out grabbing some supplies for metal shop and grabbing lunch for a few of us, anyway. Might as well say hi."

People like Chelsea Collier were one of the many reasons Kyle loved living in Marietta. Someone always ready to lend a hand. "Much appreciated, Chelsea."

"No problem. Her name was on the updated class roster they sent me yesterday. Guess they registered online."

"Thanks, Chelsea. It's a big move. I'd bet Trinity needs a friend or two before she walks in on Monday." He tossed the last bag full of painter's tape onto the driver's side seat.

"Glad to do it, Kyle. Thanks for your work on Harry's House." She patted his arm before heading inside the store.

"And Chelsea?"

"Yes?"

"I didn't ask you to do this."

She gave him a look of understanding. "You got it."

On the way back to the job site, Kyle shoved down two protein bars and a bag of cinnamon almonds, but he knew he'd be starving within the next hour. The diner came into view, but he didn't have time to stop.

Besides, she's busy. I'm busy. But rational thought had little effect on his want to stop and linger at the counter while he watched Gabriella work. Even though she'd said she wouldn't go in until Monday, he was sure she'd be there.

When he walked into the building, the delicious smell of sugar and bread hit him in the face. "What the hell?"

The others had also arrived but were crowded around one of the remaining kitchen counters.

Standing next to it, Brett pointed. "Check this out."

"What is that?" Jonah Clark asked as he shoved his cap into his back pocket.

Brett smiled like he'd won the lottery. "Dig in, boys."

Confused, Kyle approached to find a large platter of different types of cookies, chocolate-dipped pretzels, and brownies. Next to that sat a couple of loaves of sliced bread that smelled of cinnamon.

"Who brought this?" Lyle Tate lingered over the cookies before grabbing two.

The homemade sweets sat perfectly arranged on a decorative tray.

Tom Reynolds mumbled around a mouthful of something, "Holy crap. It's still warm."

"I'm gonna try these." Kurt Mayall snatched what appeared to be sugar, peanut butter, and chocolate chip cookies with nuts.

"Try these." Brett pointed to a row of bite-sized brownies

with powdered sugar and flecks of red. "I've already eaten two, but there's some sort of spice on them. They're hot."

A slow smirk spread across Kyle's face at the familiar chocolate treats.

Brownies Picantes.

"Wuss." Greedily, Kyle picked up three and shoved them whole into his mouth. The pinch of the pepper immediately burned his tongue, as he savored the layers of powdered sugar and rich chocolate that followed.

Sweet and spicy. Just like her.

Immediately, he wanted more.

"You ate three? I can do that." Brett snatched one and greedily ate it. He closed his eyes and pounded the table. "I think that one cleared my sinuses, but damn if that isn't good."

"Who brought all this?" Dan Clark asked as he picked up a handful of pretzels.

"Gabriella," Kyle managed to answer around the mouthful of brownies before his co-worker had the chance.

Brett's forehead furrowed. "Dammit, Cavasos. I was going to tell them."

"Who's Gabriella?" Gavin Clark asked after snatching another piece of what looked like banana nut bread. "Did she put cashews in this? Holy shit. This is delicious."

Brett wagged his eyebrows as he leaned against the wall. He held up a homemade card. "The new girl in town. Bought the diner from Paige."

Kyle's muscles tensed as he snatched the card away. On the front was a pencil sketch of Harry's House. *Trinity really does have a creative eye for the world.* "She and her daughter moved in next door to me. Yesterday. Her daughter probably drew this."

"I hear they're from Texas. Lotta good-looking women from Texas."

"Yee-haw." Gavin laughed as he stuffed a couple of the pretzels in his mouth.

Kyle didn't like where this conversation was headed. Instead, he'd think of some easy distraction. "Plenty of good women from Texas: Beyoncé. Summer Glau, Eva Longoria, Angie Harmon, Jennifer Garner."

"Jennifer Garner's not from Texas," Brett scoffed as he broke off part of a sugar cookie and gave it to Duke. The dog inhaled it without chewing. "She's from the East Coast."

"Born in Houston. Her parents moved to Charleston with her and her sisters when she was a kid." The only reason Kyle knew this was because of the conversation he had with the lovely actress during one of his mother's movie premieres.

"What, she tell you that?"

Kyle bit his tongue before the confession came out. Of course, none of these guys would believe him if he said yes, so what difference did it make? "Yeah, Adams. She told me when we were walking the red carpet at a movie event. Right afterward, Ben Affleck challenged me to see how many push-ups we could do."

I won by a landslide.

"You're so full of shit, Cavasos." Brett grabbed another sweet.

"Doesn't matter where she's from, this Texan lives here now and I'd expect all of us to be kind and welcoming and *respectful*," Jonah added. He gave Kyle a sideways glance.

"What? Why are you looking at me when you say that?" Brett snapped. "I can be respectful."

"You *can* be." Todd smirked.

"And you *will* be. Especially since she's here with her daughter," Kyle growled. The words came out sharper than he anticipated, but hearing Brett talk about Gabriella sounded like nails on a chalkboard. *She's way out of your league, dude.*

Brushing his hands off on his jeans, Brett smirked the way he always did when he knew he'd gotten under Kyle's skin. "What's her name again?"

"Which one?" Kyle claimed the last of the brownies. "The mother or the daughter?"

"Both."

Not that Kyle wanted to tell that jerk anything. Despite him being in charge of the K9 group and a reliable part of the first responders, his personal track record was less desirable. Brett had bragged on more than one occasion about being a love 'em and leave 'em type. Something Kyle guessed Gabriella wanted no part of or needed, especially since her ex's nickname was Peter the Cheater.

Glad my sisters don't live here. I'd refuse to let them date this guy.

"Cavasos. You gonna answer me or what?"

"The daughter's name is Trinity. The mother, Gabriella."

"Gabrrrrrriella." Brett smirked as he crossed his feet at the ankles. "She's a looker for sure."

"Yep, she is." *Back off, buddy.* Not that Kyle thought he had cornered the market when it came to his new neighbor, but the idea of Brett's hands all over Gabriella's café au lait colored skin caused Kyle's frustration to simmer under the surface.

Gabriella didn't need that kind of heartbreak.

Lyle jumped in. "She bought the diner. I wondered what Paige was planning to do with it."

"If she cooks anything else half as good as this stuff, I'm gonna be over there a whole lot more." Jonah blissed out on the last sugar cookie.

"Might have to go visit the diner more myself." Brett wagged his eyebrows as Duke nudged his owner's arm, apparently wanting more sweets.

Anger still simmered under the surface. "She's not your type." The harsh words escaped him. For whatever reason, Brett always did have a knack for annoying Kyle.

The jovial mood between the men vanished.

Brett stood, his hands on his hips. "What's my type,

Cavasos?"

"You mean more than breathing, Adams?" Kurt leaned against the bare stud of the former wall.

A collective chuckle from the rest of the crew, but all watched the men's exchange with cautious looks.

Despite the devil-may-care attitude, the muscles in Brett's jaw clenched. "More than breathing."

Kyle didn't answer. It wasn't worth getting into a fight with the meathead. Besides, why make things complicated when family obligations might pull Kyle out of Marietta anyway?

His stomach twisted at that possibility. He didn't want to be pulled back into that drama.

"You got something to say to me, Cavasos?"

Before anger got the better of him, Kyle pointed at his watch. "We've got work to do."

All the men reluctantly agreed and Kyle rattled off each of their instructions for the latter half of the day.

He sent Brett off with Lyle to start putting up the drywall in the upstairs rooms.

Before each got back to it, every single one of them grabbed a final sweet.

"Don't let him get to you." Jonah patted his friend on the back after helping him unload supplies. "Even though you got it bad."

Chapter Ten

"VANILLA, FLOUR, SUGAR, cinnamon…" Gabriella called out the diner kitchen's inventory as Trinity checked things off the carefully created list.

Her daughter tapped the iPad screen with each ingredient. "Got it. Got it. Got it. Pepper?"

"Yes, seasoned salt. Lemon pepper?" Reaching around a large container of salt, Gabriella found an almost empty bottle of one of her favorite spices. "Here it is. We'll need more."

"Got it."

"There's six fifty-pound bags of flour, seven thirty-pound bags of sugar, five bags of baking soda…"

As the lunch rush began to die down, Gabriella continued to go through her binder of instructions Paige had given her about the diner, as she watched the crew out of the corner of her eye.

"Why are we up here, Gabby?" Trinity yawned. "You don't even start until Monday."

"Because I want to see what is here and what we need. Plus it helped us get the food done for the guys faster than if we'd baked at home. The ovens are bigger here." Checking the date on a bottle of vanilla, she continued. "And I get to see the flow of the staff, work the breakfast rush, and meet the regular customers. It's been a productive morning."

She planned to come in and watch things as a customer, but after Kyle introduced her last night, it was impossible to watch as an unknown observer.

Because she'd spent most of the night having erotic dreams about her neighbor, she'd gotten little sleep and it kept her restless for most of the morning. A hard day's work would certainly help quell that flutter of excitement when hearing his name.

If he's half as good in my dreams as he is in real life, I'm in so much trouble. Her body tingled at the replay of her stripping off his shirt, before he unbuttoned his jeans, allowing them to slowly slide to the floor and... *And I'm more than happy to be in that kind of trouble.*

"Come on. Let's walk around the town. Or let's go to Bozeman. Get some art supplies." A heavy sigh from Trinity yanked Gabriella out of her daydreams.

"Sweetie, let me get this done and hopefully we can go later today." Gabriella shivered at the remaining images of her saucy thoughts.

Running her fingers through her hair, she pursed her lips. "Do you think it'll be better here? I mean, do you think I'll get bullied...again?"

Her daughter's worry-soaked words stopped Gabriella in

her tracks. She put down the binder and pulled her child into her arms. "I think it's going to be amazingly better for so many reasons."

"Marietta is a great place to live, sweetheart," Flo chimed in. "Plus, if someone's bullying you, they can't keep it a secret. Everyone's gonna know and we've got a lot of good kids here."

Trinity sniffed. "I'm scared, Gabby."

She's still calling me Gabby. What did her aunt say to her? "Change can be scary, but think of the new adventures here. There are plenty of places to hike, plus you get to learn to ski, snowboard."

"And ice-skate."

"Ice-skate. Really?" That made the girl sit up and take notice. "Where?"

"Over on Miracle Lake. It's cold, but it's fun." Tapping her chin, the waitress cocked her head. "If I recall correctly, Freddie is pretty good on skates. I think he likes hockey."

"Hockey's...good."

Drying her daughter's tears with her thumbs, Gabriella coaxed, "It's gonna be good here."

The sadness in Trinity's big brown eyes was a kick in the gut. *All because of one shitty boss.*

Despite presenting a strong front, Riley Fitzgerald's wicked smirk only drove Gabriella's frustration higher. *How dare he let his daughter terrorize mine because I wouldn't keep my mouth shut about what he'd done.*

Last night when Kyle asked why she hadn't reported Riley's actions to upper management, Gabriella wanted to confess it all, but she stopped herself.

Not even Trinity knew the entire story. As stressed as her daughter had been over the last few weeks, the last thing she wanted was to upset her more. "We're good?"

"We're good." Trinity tapped the iPad. "Butter. Eggs. Napkins?"

Flo leaned against the wall next to the shelves. Her hot pink dice earrings swayed by her cheeks. "Lunch rush is about over. Need help with anything?"

If the woman hadn't been so kind from the get-go, Gabriella would have assumed it was all an act, but Flo was the real deal. "I have a question for you, Flo. These are the standard spices y'all use?"

The corner of Flo's mouth curled down. "What do you mean standard?"

"Basic stock. Staples."

"Pretty much. Why?"

"Just asking, really. Wondering about adding a few things to the menu."

She pursed her lips. "What kind of things?"

Careful, Gabby. She knows this place like the back of her hand. "Not sure yet. Anything you'd like to see?"

Her eyes went wide. "Oh, I'd have to think about it."

"What about local farmers? I see a few jars of honey on the shelves. Are those from a local farm?" Trinity pointed.

"Yes, Austin and Melinda Sweet bought a place here a while back. Make organic honey. I bought a few jars not too long ago to serve here. They grow some vegetables. Have chickens."

"Chickens? Can we buy our eggs from them?" Gabriella grabbed the binder off the counter. Flipping through it, she finally found the page she needed. "Yes, Austin and Melinda Sweet. Paige wrote it down."

"You wanna buy from locals?"

"Of course. Why wouldn't I?"

A wide smile spread across her hot pink lips. "They won't have enough to keep us fully stocked, but it's more than they can eat for sure."

"I like that. Would you be willing to introduce me to them? Since you know everybody, seems you would be a great person to be in charge of this." Gabriella's heart pounded ninety-to-nothing, hoping the olive branch she'd extended would be enough to lessen the loyal employee's worry.

"I'll see what I can do, but I'm sure they'd love to feed the masses."

"And I'd be glad to design a sign saying we're using their eggs." Trinity snapped her fingers.

Mentally patting herself on the back, Gabriella added, "Thank you, Flo. Bringing in local businesses, ranchers, farmers, is a brilliant move."

A flash of pink appeared on Flo's pretty cheeks. "Hear

that, Griffin? I'm brilliant."

"Already knew that," the cook called out from the kitchen. Today, they'd had the pleasure of meeting the second cook, Griffin.

He and his brother Merlin were very similar in size, but where Merlin had darker hair, Griffin's was lighter. Both appeared to like 1980s rock and both had been loyal employees.

Gabriella thanked her lucky stars that they'd stayed on and been nothing but friendly.

Trinity snapped her fingers as if she'd remembered something. "Speaking of using local farmers. Back home, I mean, back in Texas, we have this big grocery store chain called HEB and they work directly with farmers, ranchers, fishermen. It's made a huge difference in community partnerships."

"How so?" Flo asked as she wiped down a few salt and pepper shakers.

Trinity added, giving Gabriella a quick wink, "People are more likely to shop at HEB if they know the company supports local businesses."

Glad to know when it comes down to it, my daughter's still on my side. Gabriella wondered how long that would last. Would Trinity go through her rebellious teen years like her own mother had?

Flo looked back and forth between the two women. "Well, that does make sense. I'm sure come spring, the

Sweets would be more than happy to sell some of their fresh vegetables too. You might also want to talk to Chad Anders. He helped the Sweets get their farm up and running."

"Great idea." Gabriella considered this a supervisor's victory. Her phone chimed, signaling the last loaf of cinnamon bread was ready. "Oh, good. We can get this done and get home."

"Might as well get this place put back together since the lunch crowd's gone." Flo grabbed a broom and danced out to the dining room.

"She's fun." Trinity smirked. "I bet she's got great stories."

"I have no doubt. Paige said Flo's been here for years. Knows the place backwards and forwards."

"I wonder why she didn't try and sell the diner to Flo."

"Hard to say." Gabriella placed the bread on a cooling rack and slid the entire thing into the freezer. "What do you say, orange glaze?"

Trinity jumped up and headed for the pantry. "I get to lick the spoon."

Setting the timer, Gabriella pulled a small bowl off the shelf as Trinity brought the powdered sugar, an orange, and vanilla.

"You want to make it this time?"

A slow smile spread across Trinity's face. "Really?"

"Go for it."

"Order from the teachers at the high school, Griffin,"

Casey handed the slip through the kitchen window to the cook. "Said they'd be by in about ten to pick it up."

"Got it." He spun the order wheel and grabbed the slip as it whipped by. The radio on the upper shelf played 1980s rock and the first bars of Def Leppard's "Animal" came on.

As the cook threw some bread on the grill, his head bounced along with the beat of the music.

Gabriella smiled at the man's perpetual good mood.

"Gabby, is this right? A cup of powdered sugar, a few drips of vanilla, and to start, a teaspoon of fresh-squeezed orange juice."

"Exactly."

As they'd done since Trinity was able to walk, the two stood side by side while creating something amazing.

Trinity mumbled instructions as she worked. Little by little, she blended the orange juice in until the glaze looked like a white, silky river.

Within minutes, the fresh smell of citrus-laced sugar drifted about the room, making Gabriella's mouth water. She dipped a small spoon in and tasted. "Perfect."

Her daughter's face lit up. "Really?"

The timer pinged. "I'll get the bread." Gabriella pulled the loaf from the freezer and placed it on the counter. Resting her hand on the bread, Gabriella nodded. "Perfectly chilled. You want to do the icing or do you want me to do it?"

"Me!" Drizzling the icing over the bread, Trinity created

intricate long strings of a sugar design. By the time she was done, the bread looked like someone had decorated it with glistening white lace. Motioning to Trinity, Gabriella took the dessert. "You get to lick the spoon."

"Orange icing, yummy," her daughter practically squealed.

Slicing the dessert into small cubes, Gabriella placed the bite-size bits into mini cupcake paper cups.

The swinging doors flew open as Flo entered carrying a few dishes and the broom. She inhaled. "Goodness, something smells wonderful."

"I thought we could have samples of things we might add to the menu. No point in making something that no one will eat."

Casey came in backward, pushing the double doors with her back. As she turned around, she held a large bin, overflowing with dirty dishes. "Thanks for holding the door for me, Flo."

Trinity jumped up and offered to help carry the bin, which Casey immediately accepted. "Something smells good."

"It's cinnamon bread with orange glaze," Trinity replied as the slam of the heavy bin echoed from the sink.

"Thank you for helping, T." With Flo hovering next to her, Gabriella's heart rate skyrocketed.

The bread would be the first thing she'd ask the staff to try.

Please be good. "I'm trying to see what people like, don't like. Make smaller portions and hand out free samples."

"Free samples?" Flo knowingly nodded. "If you're gonna hand out free stuff, I'm sure plenty of people will be more than happy to eat it."

"Exactly, Flo. Hopefully, this will be good enough to make them come back."

Griffin sauntered up. "If it smells as good as it tastes, people are gonna like it and buy plenty."

Holding the tray up, Gabriella encouraged everyone to take a sample. "See what you think."

"No, I'm fine. Thanks, guys," Casey snarked as she entered again with another bin full of dishes. "I've got this heavy bin of dishes taken care of. Don't worry about me."

"Good Lord, girl. You don't get a medal for everything. It's called work for a reason." Flo took a sample. As soon as it touched her tongue her face lit up. "That's good."

"Thank you, Flo." *Score one for me.*

Griffin took two samples and Casey helped herself as well. All of them nodded in approval.

Flo took one more. "We'll hand these out for the rest of the day. See what the general consensus is."

Mission accomplished. "Thank you, Flo. We'll get out of your hair now. Thank you for letting us use the kitchen for the snack trays."

She placed a gentle hand on Gabriella's arm. "I'm sure the guys appreciated it. That was a right nice thing for you to do."

"Kyle said the house is for a fallen first responder?"

"Yes, such a good man. Harry Monroe always had a smile on his face and a song in his heart." The waitress wiped away a tear. "Those boys are doing a great thing by him."

Casey rolled her eyes. "That reminds me, I've got to go pick up Duke when I finish. Brett said he's bored."

"Knock, knock." A lovely blond-haired woman waved at them through the kitchen pass-through window.

Flo motioned for her to come on back. "Hey there, Chelsea. Need a lunch to go?"

"Yes, Flo." She walked straight up to Trinity and extended her hand. "You must be Trinity. I'm Chelsea Collier. I teach history at the high school."

"Oh. Nice to meet you, Miss Collier." Trinity responded in kind. "This is my…this is Gabriella. I hang out with her."

Teenagers. Gabriella plastered on her best mom smile. "I'm Trinity's mom. Nice to meet you."

"I heard through the grapevine we had a new student. I wanted to come by and welcome you to Marietta."

"How lovely. Thank you," said Gabriella.

With a sideways glance at her mother, Trinity motioned toward a table. "Thanks, Miss Collier. Would you like to sit down?"

"Your order will be ready in about five minutes, Chelsea," Griffin called through the kitchen window.

"Sure. That would be nice."

"Give her a sample. Show off your icing." Gabriella whispered, hoping to encourage the girl to talk to her new instructor.

"Good idea." Trinity pointed to the dining room after grabbing a couple of samples of the cinnamon bread. "Try this. I made the icing."

"Thank you."

Flo went into the back to get a few things as Gabriella helped Casey to finish cleaning the dining room and wash the dishes.

By the time Miss Collier left, Trinity appeared to be in a less anxious mood.

The teacher's visit helped establish some high hopes that the rest of the day would continue on the upswing.

Before they donned their new jackets, Flo pulled Gabriella aside. "Sweetie, that's a nice thing you did for the boys, but I don't want you to get hurt."

"What are you talking about?"

"I know he brought you two in last night, but Kyle hasn't been in town that long. Best I can tell, he keeps to himself. Quiet man. Hasn't asked anyone out since he's been here so please don't get a broken heart if him bringing you in last night was only a friendly welcome."

Buttoning up her coat, Gabriella bit her lip to keep herself from describing the scorchingly hot *welcome* kiss they'd shared last night. "I'll keep that in mind, Flo. Thank you."

The women ran to their car and quickly got out of the

cold.

Trinity pulled out her phone and immediately began to ignore her mother. Gabriella decided a nice distraction for herself would be to drive by Harry's House and see how well the job had come along.

That doesn't scream needy at all. Get a grip.

When the light at Second and Church turned red, it took everything Gabriella had not to stop in and check on the guys doing the renovations. She'd been disappointed that Kyle wasn't there when she and Trinity brought the treats, but that wasn't why she'd delivered them.

Well, it wasn't the only reason.

Being the new girl in town, she knew there would be a decent amount of uncertainty about what she would bring, especially to a central hub like the Main Street Diner. She hoped her gesture of sweets and protein-filled snacks would bring some of these guys into the diner sooner rather than later.

Brett, Casey's brother, had been nice, but his brash personality rubbed her the wrong way. Plus, his eyes lingered on her boobs a bit too much.

Keep driving. They're busy. They don't have time to visit.

Casually, she glanced to her left to see all the men working in the sweet A-Frame house. Despite the chilly air, the ones she could see though the window had on short sleeves or sleeveless shirts.

I wonder what Kyle looks like in a sleeveless shirt.
Shirtless.

Pantsless.

A wave of heat wrapped around her like a warm blanket.

As Trinity frantically texted, Gabriella craned her neck to see Kyle, but no such luck.

Out of the corner of her eye, movement caught her attention. Looking up to the second floor, she saw Brett giving her a wave and a smile as he held a window in place while another guy worked around him.

She gave an obligatory nod before turning.

Within minutes, they were home and Trinity jumped out of the car before the engine was off.

"If the roads don't freeze, tomorrow we'll head out by nine, okay? That should put us in Bozeman around ten." Gabriella called out to Trinity as the teen took the stairs two at a time. "Give us plenty of time to shop without being in a hurry."

"Sounds good. I'll be in my room." Cookie ran up the stairs, hot on the teen's heels. The international signal of "do not disturb" echoed through the house with the click of the lock on Trinity's bedroom door.

"Um, okay. Sure." A nugget of sadness settled in Gabriella's heart watching her daughter grow up.

It wasn't that Gabriella didn't want to see her daughter's accomplishments, but did she have to grow up so fast?

The rhythmic thud-thud-thud of Belle's tail hitting the chair made Gabriella smile. The old dog slowly stood then turned around and walked into the kitchen. "Need to go outside, girl?"

Once the dog had taken care of business and her paws were dried, Gabriella changed into her favorite pajama shorts and put on the sweater Kyle gave to her the night before.

The soft, tight-knit fabric warmed her immediately and she couldn't help but think of how gallantly he'd found warm clothing for them just to go to dinner. That alone warmed her body in unexpected ways.

And all this time I thought good men had disappeared. Chivalry isn't dead. It's just hiding in Montana.

Still, a donated Burberry sweater? It looked practically brand-new. From the looks of the town, Gabriella searched her brain as to where these kinds of donations had come from.

But her mental search didn't last long. Her exhausted body and brain urged her to sit and relax for a bit.

With it only being four in the afternoon, Gabriella expected full sun, but the sun set a bit earlier here. The long shadows of the late day had already cast over the yard and the bare-branched trees. Looking out her kitchen window, she watched a dark line of clouds brew over the mountain range as Trinity shuffled in wearing her oversized unicorn house shoes. "What is that again, Coppertop Mountain?"

"I dunno. Something like that." Yawning, the teen prepared a mug of hot chocolate, filling the container to the rim with mini marshmallows.

"Guess we should get used to snowstorms. Nothing like

that back in Lone Star Crossing." Settling back in the wobbly kitchen chair, Gabriella shivered at the idea of having to dig a path to her car from her front porch before sunrise. "Do we even have a shovel? Or salt for the front porch steps?"

"No clue. I haven't checked the garage." A slow smirk spread across her daughter's face before she popped the handle down on the K-Cup machine. "But I bet Kyle does and I'm sure he'd *love* to help you figure all that out."

Just the mention of the man's name made Gabriella's face hot, but she tried to answer as casually as she could. "I'm sure he does. He's been here over a year."

The low hum of the machine heating the water echoed through the kitchen as Trinity leaned against the counter. "That blush across your cheeks suits you, Gabby."

A giggle escaped her. "I don't know what you're talking about."

"Right and I'm the Queen of England."

"England would be privileged to call you their queen."

"Wouldn't that be something? A woman of color, the Queen of England?" Trinity mimicked putting a crown on her head. "I could give that Meghan Markle a run for her money."

"Only after you're eighteen."

"You think Harry would wait that long for me?"

"He's a fool if he doesn't."

"Thanks." She popped the handle up and tossed the K-

Cup in the trash. A gooey line of melted sugar dripped over the side of the mug and ran down to stick to the paper towel Trinity placed underneath it.

The smell of chocolate made Gabriella's mouth water. "Is there any more?"

Nodding, Trinity placed another serving into the machine and started it up. "Sure. Let me make it for you."

"That would be nice." Gabriella stood next to her daughter and Trinity rested her head on her mother's shoulder as they watched the hot water drip into the class of 2005 Lone Star Crossing High School mug.

Despite not being biologically related to her, Gabriella had always thought of herself as Trinity's mother. It was happy moments like these when that reinforced her protective mama-bear instinct and she knew she'd made the right choice of taking over the girl's care.

A gust of wind blew by, shaking the windows and sending the few leaves still around high into the air. "Guess that means the storm isn't far behind. Probably won't make it to Bozeman tomorrow."

"Probably not, but it's an adventure, right? For us."

A loud snore made them both jump. They turned to see Belle asleep by one of the floor vents, the warm air playing with the old dog's thick fur.

Trinity giggled. "Looks like Belle found her spot."

The way the girl laughed reminded Gabriella so much of her best friend, Laurie. Her green eyes and her long, elegant fingers were copies of her mother's. Sadly, her beautiful skin color had been what decided who cared for her since Laurie's husband and her family had no interest in "that" child.

How can people be so cruel?

"How many marshmallows, Gabby?"

"A handful would be great."

After dropping the sugary goodness in, Trinity picked up her mug and headed out. She paused in the doorway and turned. "Everyone says hi back in Texas."

"Is that who you were texting?"

"Yes." With one beautiful long finger, she traced the rim of her mug as she lingered.

Sadness settled in Gabriella's stomach. "I'm sorry I couldn't make the bullying stop. I tried; I truly did."

"Believe me, Sheila would announce it in the hallways every time she'd been reprimanded by the principal because *my* mom couldn't stop blabbing."

"Good grief. You couldn't win no matter what you did. What I did." Shaking her head, Gabriella wished she'd had as much influence as her adversary, Riley, or his rich friends seemed to. *Still, I keep thinking I should report this. He's got to be hurting business.* "I keep thinking if I had been stronger or more demanding or richer or—"

"Don't do that to yourself." Pulling up a chair, Trinity sat across from her. "You're one of the best people I know."

Her daughter's unexpected praise caused Gabriella's vision to blur. She quickly wiped away her tears. "I just want so much for you, T. So much more than I had or your mom had."

"Can you tell me another story about her?"

The request triggered an unexpected wave of tears. It took Gabriella a moment to collect herself. "Sorry, I ... You haven't asked in so long about your mom."

"Guess I've had my mind on other things." Trinity's hand gently rested on Gabriella's arm. "Another story. Please."

"Your mom could solve every puzzle on *Wheel of Fortune* with less than a third of it uncovered. She loved Mad Libs and chocolate sundaes and rollerblading."

"What else?" Leaning in, Trinity's wide-eyed enthusiasm only encouraged Gabriella.

"She loved singing, but she wasn't very good at it. She'd always mix up the lyrics. I remember one time, we were trying to go to sleep and your mom kept singing a song... What was it?" Tapping her front teeth, Gabriella searched her brain until she grabbed the memory with both hands. An instant giggle emerged. "She kept singing a line in that Bon Jovi song 'Living on a Prayer' when they sing something like it doesn't make a difference if we make or not."

"And what did my mom sing?"

The sweet memory kept Gabriella laughing so hard, she could barely get the words out. "Laurie kept singing, 'it doesn't make a difference if we're naked or not.'"

"Those aren't the words at all." Trinity held her stomach

as she laughed. "Oh, my gosh. That's funny."

"I know, but she wouldn't listen to me. We played that song over and over again and she heard one set of lyrics and I heard another. We never did agree on what they were singing."

As the laughter died down, Trinity grabbed her mother's hand. "Thanks, Gabby. Thanks for being there for my mom."

"Of course." Wiping her tears of joy away, she squeezed her daughter's hand. "I'm happy to do it."

Chapter Eleven

As soon as Trinity took her hot chocolate upstairs to read, Angelica Marcos's picture popped up on Gabriella's phone as it rang.

For the first time ever, Gabriella wished the other person on the line was a pushy telemarketer. "Hello, Mama."

"You make the trip okay?"

"*Sí,* it wasn't bad. Just a sucky long drive."

"Language, *mija,* language." Angelica Marcos's stern voice made Gabriella sit up straight and square her shoulders.

"It was a long drive, but it's really pretty here."

"Cold?"

"Very."

"How's my granddaughter? She happy to be away from that terrible girl?" The growl in her mother's voice mimicked her own.

"I think the distance has helped Trinity relax a bit. She met one of her teachers today." She took a sip of the hot chocolate. The creamy sweetness coated her tongue as the wind howled.

"You're staying. For sure?"

"I'm staying." *Because I honestly have no other choice right now.*

"Don't you think Mr. Riley would give you your job back if you asked? You make so many families happy with your food."

If you only knew the entire story. She hadn't said a word to her family about the demands from her former boss. Her mother would blow her top if she knew. "Mom, I wanted my own place to grow. I'd done all I could there at Winston."

Knowing she'd saved her family's jobs gave her peace of mind and that she could live with, as long as Riley kept his word.

A few sniffs came through before her mother sobbed, "But I miss you so much. I don't see your faces every day."

"I know, Mama. I miss you, too." Hearing her mother's voice immediately triggered a deep longing for home.

The low rumble of the heat kicking on reminded her of the frigid weather outside.

The overcast day was no spring in Texas. There were no flowers. No green on the trees. No warmth in the air. No bluebonnets.

Like it or not, it's home now.

Her eyes drifted to the house next door. Through her kitchen window she could see Kyle's lights were still dark, but her heart fluttered at the possibility of getting to know him better.

"Mama. Trust me, *por favor?*"

"I do, *mija*, but Montana is a long, long way."

Taking a travel-sized bottle of chocolate tequila out of the cabinet, she gave herself a three-second pour into her mug. "But it's going to be good."

"I don't like this, I don't see you every day, but you are a good girl. Raise your daughter. Get her to finish school." Her mother gave a long sigh. "Tell me what's so great about Montana."

As Belle snored and Gabriella sipped her spiked hot chocolate, she told her mother of the mountains, the town, the community service the first responders were doing on Harry's House all while carefully omitting one particular person, not that it mattered.

"Trinity tells me your new neighbor is nice. *Está buenísimo!*"

Hearing her mother talk about her "hot" neighbor, made Gabriella laugh. "*Sí.*"

"And his last name is Cavasos. Good Spanish name." The smile in Angelica's voice permeated the distance between them.

Great. My mother is monitoring my social life from over a thousand miles away.

"Yes, he's nice." *And I hope he's a bit naughty too.* When her mother didn't scream at her over the phone about how good girls don't say things like that, Gabriella breathed a sigh of relief she hadn't said it out loud. "He's been very helpful to us."

"Trinity told me. He bring you food and show you the town. And Cookie *gatita* likes him. Sounds like a good man. You should marry him."

"*Virgen Santa!* Mama, I've known him one day. People don't get married after one day." But she had to admit that him passing the Cookie cat test was a big positive in his favor.

"I think he sound like someone you should marry."

"I'll let him know, Mama. I love you."

"*Te amo, mija.* I talk to you soon. Bye."

Through the window, she could see Kyle's house still remained dark. She wondered when he'd be home, if he could use a hot meal after working all day at Harry's House… *Get hold of yourself. You've known him a day. One. Day.*

Yet, the possibility of getting to *know* Kyle Cavasos tickled her ovaries more than it ever did the entire five years she dated her former fiancé, Derrick, or as Trinity liked to call him, Peter the Cheater.

That man's act of betrayal angered her beyond measure. *All he had to do was call it off. Instead, he gets pregnant with some other woman and still doesn't have the balls to tell me.*

Hearing the news from her mother had to be one of the worst ego punches Gabriella had ever encountered. Worse than losing her first baking contest.

Worse than being told she wasn't pretty enough to be in

the high school's musical.

And worse than realizing her boss had stolen several of her recipes and passed them off as his own.

Secret-keeping had always been a deal breaker for Gabriella, especially when it involved family and her heart.

Her eyes betrayed her, glancing over to the neighbor's house again.

Stop it. You'll make yourself crazy and the last thing you need is to be the crazy lady who lives next to the hot guy.

Shaking off her lustful ideas, she decided making him something quick would take the edge off. She poured it into a smaller container and then inside a small cooler bag before braving the cold and placing it on his front doorstep.

It took a good five minutes of her huddled under a thick blanket for her to stop shivering. By the time the chill broke, exhaustion set in and she decided a short nap would be the best course of action to reset her brain and body.

To keep from sleeping too long, she opened the front curtains to soak up as much sunshine as she could, but the gray skies offered little in the way of natural light. A fine cloud of dust danced around her, making her sneeze. "Ugh, well, guess I'll add vacuuming to the to-do list."

Fatigue begged for her to lie down. "I'll clean house later."

Instead, she snuggled in on the couch and tried to read her back issues of *Cook's Illustrated*, *Fine Cooking*, and the trashy *US Weekly* Trinity convinced her to buy in Billings.

Glancing at the cover of Jason Crowe cheating on his latest wife, she shook her head. "Jeez, I guess money doesn't buy happiness or fidelity. What a jerk."

But something about him caught her attention. She looked closer. The chiseled jaw and profile reminded her of her neighbor. "Trinity was right. Kyle does look a bit like him."

She tossed the magazine on the coffee table. "Thank goodness he's no relation because I'd dump any relative of his in a hot second."

Pulling her favorite blanket to her chest, Gabriella flipped through the cooking magazines again, hoping to find some new ideas, but her thoughts stuck like peanut butter on the guy next door and his more than impressive biceps.

After seeing what the group had already accomplished this morning, Gabriella had full confidence they'd reach their deadline. The ripped-out drywall already made the place look more spacious and welcoming. The double-paned windows would certainly warm the place up. He'd taken her advice about removing the cabinets and stripping them down.

The space heaters they'd brought in only took off the chill in the building, but add in some new insulation and the place should be plenty warm in these Montana winters.

Of course as excited as Gabriella was when she walked into the building, she could have heated the entire place to summertime in Texas temperatures. The mere hope of getting a glimpse of Kyle all sweaty from a hard day's work had her this side of spontaneous combustion.

Plus, him knowing which end of a hammer to use and how to break a sweat had been other reasons that kept her up most of the night.

Growing up in a family where you were expected to perform simple home repairs, Gabby expected a man to know as much as she did when it came to your basic toolbox.

She had little patience for men who barely knew how to change a lightbulb or those who didn't understand the difference between a flathead or Phillips-head screwdriver.

Like Derrick.

What did I ever see in that guy?

Shaking off her frustration, she tried to focus on an article about kitchen equipment reviews, but after a few minutes, the magazine fell from her fingers as she drifted off to sleep.

Chapter Twelve

KYLE COULDN'T HAVE been happier with what everyone had accomplished in these past twelve hours. He'd pushed the guys hard, but they'd been able to get all the toilets changed out, the walls ripped out and put up, the kitchen counters ripped out, and the cabinet fronts removed. All the windows were installed and, next week, he'd get the insulation in so they wouldn't have to use the space heaters.

He'd even checked that all the aluminum wiring had been removed and the copper had been run. He had everything lined up for when he returned to change out the fuse box, getting it connected and up to code.

Even the building inspector came by and remarked how Kyle and the men had done a great job. They would have no trouble passing inspection if this kept up.

Hearing that gave everyone a well-deserved pick-me-up at the end of a long day's work.

Even Brett looked pleased with his work in the bathrooms. Of course, Kyle went behind him afterward to make sure the seals were in place and the toilets were installed properly.

Driving the short way home—replaying all of that—only made the day better, but the moment Kyle's mood went from pleased to ecstatic was when he drove straight down 3rd Street and saw the light on in Gabriella's front room.

She's home. She's awake.

Every minute, she'd been in the back of his mind. Her smile. Her sense of humor. The way she looked in that damned red sweater.

What I wouldn't give to rip that sweater off her curvy body.

His fierce libido made him chuckle. He wouldn't deny his attraction to her, but he knew a long time ago he'd never be the love 'em and leave 'em type.

Otherwise, you're just Jason Crowe all over again.

And he'd be damned if he'd be anything like that man.

As he drove into his driveway, he noticed something on his front porch.

He quickly unloaded his truck, packing everything back into the garage. Entering from the back door, he placed his father's precious toolbox in the kitchen cabinet right as his phone beeped.

Angrily, he jerked it out of his belt holder, but his frustrations calmed when Charlie's name popped up. She needed his top three choices for the calendar photos.

He spread the pictures on the far kitchen counter and made his selections. His favorite had his face partially covered, but his famous jawline and smile exposed.

As much as he hated to admit it, the photo shoot hadn't

been terrible. In fact, looking at these, Kyle patted himself on the back for his early morning workouts and his commitment to staying in shape.

After a quick text back to Charlie, he shifted gears and tossed the lemon chicken into the oven along with a couple of baked potatoes. He ran by the front door to clean up and get presentable, and then he remembered the bag.

He snatched it from the cold and inside was a note and a container. He read the note out loud. "T told me you hadn't had this in a while. I hope it's as good as you remember. Enjoy. From your new neighbors."

Popping the top, the flavors of onions, tomatoes, cilantro, citrus, garlic, and peppers flowed out and attacked his nostrils.

"*Pico de Gallo.*" Kyle moaned and inhaled again. "Damn, this is good. I'm gonna have to tell her thank you."

Placing the food in the refrigerator, he showered and dressed in record time.

It's good manners to give an in-person thank-you, right?

He laughed at himself. If he were honest, he'd simply admit he wanted to see her again. And again. And again.

That alone made him uneasy. Relationships had always been challenging when you were from Hollywood royalty. Never knowing if a woman wanted to be with you or with the idea of you and your family.

But here in Marietta. Here, he could simply be Kyle Cavasos, first responder and handyman and now calendar model.

Checking his breath a third time, he donned his jacket and headed over.

The temperatures dropped rapidly as the clouds moved in. They'd probably get several inches of snow tonight, slowing down the morning commute for a few outside of town and anyone trying to leave. The wind whipped around him as he sprinted across Gabriella's lawn.

Running up the steps, he slipped, but caught himself before he fell. "She needs some salt."

Looking up, he saw Gabriella, sleeping on the couch. Her dark hair falling around her face, one shapely leg uncovered and on top of a large pink blanket.

Wicked ideas bombarded his brain as his eyes ran up and down her naked leg. He licked his lips at the thought of kissing the insides of her knee, her thighs, her... *Be a gentleman.*

Shaking the ideas out of his head for the moment, he gently knocked on the door and gave her a few moments to answer as the brutal winds kicked it up a notch.

Glancing through the window, he saw she still slept. Disappointment set in. As much as he wanted to spend time with her, he figured she had to be exhausted. The drive alone would wear most out and she'd been going ninety-to-nothing since she arrived.

As he turned to leave, Andy Grammer's "Honey I'm Good" blasted from inside. Apparently, it was her phone, which jerked her awake.

With her hair in her face, she felt around for her phone before sitting up. When she did, she noticed him and smiled as she answered the phone. She held up an index finger as she made her way to the door and motioned him to come in.

"Yes, Mama. *No me voy a congelar,* it's fine. Yes, it's snowing. I'm pretty sure I can handle…*si ya se*…I don't have a shovel…*Que sí! Sí traigo guantes, gorro, y bufanda*…"

Guess, her mother is watching the weather channel. Kyle bit his lip, listening to Gabriella lie about having gloves and a good hat. *At least she had a warm coat.*

"*Que si puedo, Ma! Damn un segundo, porfa!*" She covered the phone. "Sorry, give me a second. I'm wrapping this up."

"No problem." *Keep talking Spanish.*

"Make yourself at home. I'll be right back." She disappeared into the kitchen.

The front room looked pretty much the same as it had yesterday. A few more boxes were unpacked, several framed photos were placed throughout the room, but other than that, little progress had been made.

A slow tap-tap approached. Kyle watched the old dog's lumbersome gait as she entered, tail wagging.

"Hello, Belle." He scratched the dog behind her ears and she groaned, leaning against his leg. "That feel good?"

"*Por favor cálmate mamá.* Calm down. Mom. Please. I won't get trapped in the snow. Yes, I have plenty of food. *Papel de baño.*"

Kyle bit back his laughter at the comment about toilet paper.

A couple of photographs within arm's reach caught his attention. What looked like Gabriella and several other people smiling and throwing their hands out like they'd ended a musical number. He noticed her immediately. A few others appeared to have similar facial features to hers. "Must be her family."

As he began to put down the frame, something grabbed his interest.

The sign behind them. It took him about two seconds to realize exactly what sign it was. He mumbled, "Jewel of the Hill Country, Winston Resort and Spa."

He cringed at the idea of having to leave Marietta, but giving up that kind of money would be foolish. The freedom alone it would offer was beyond what most could even hope for.

The beep of the phone turning off caught his attention. He tried to put the picture frame back before she entered, but she arched her back as she yawned. The red sweater clung to her body more than it had a right to.

The concern about being stealthy evaporated. "No, no problem. Just looking."

"That's when I started working there." She picked up the picture and pointed. "That's my brother, Edwardo, the one I mentioned who's good with fixing anything. My sisters, Maria and Helena, my cousins Raul and Reina, my mom,

Angelica, she runs the hair salon in the spa."

"You all have the same smile."

"I guess so." Tapping the far right of the picture, she finished, "Another brother, Joaquin. He's a miracle worker with plants. Got botany and landscape architecture degrees from Texas A&M. My other brother, Sergio, runs a gym and my sister, Helena, is still in school."

"A lot of you worked there."

"They all still do. It's close to the house. For my cousin, Reina, it works well with her kids' schedules. The schools are good." A hint of sadness in her voice. She put the picture down without setting it upright. "What's up? Did you get a lot done for restoration day?"

"Yes, yes we did and thank you for bringing all that food by. The guys ate it right up."

Her eyes sparkled. "I'm so glad. And you got your *Pico*?"

"Yes, thank you." They stood in awkward silence, until Kyle remembered why he came by. "Sorry, I wondered if you'd like to come over and have dinner…with me."

"That would be nice. Let me see if Trinity's up for it. She might be sleeping."

"If this is a bad time."

She waved her hands in front of her face. "No, absolutely not. She's kind of out of whack. Teenage angst."

"I remember giving my parents plenty of grief at that age." *Stop talking about your family!* Still, something about her made him want to lay his fears on the table and hope she still liked him for it.

"It's been interesting today. Productive, but interesting."

"If she's not up to joining us, I've got enough for you to take a plate home to her if you want."

"That's really sweet of you. Thank you." She ran her fingers through her hair and patted her makeup-free cheeks. "Yes, that would be lovely."

"Great. I'll go get the rest of it ready."

"Give me about twenty minutes to clean up? I'll be over."

"Perfect, but bring Trinity if she's up to it." Although, if Kyle were honest, he hoped the teen would stay home. It was a lot harder to talk to someone when their child was there.

"Sounds good."

He headed back with the help of a strong gust of wind at his back. The clouds had already made it over Copper Mountain and the snow should be falling any minute.

By the time Gabriella arrived, the first flakes began to stick. A few had ended up in her hair.

She removed her gloves and jacket to reveal the red sweater he'd given her. "Brrrrr, it's cold out there."

"About to get colder." *But it just got hot in here. Damn, woman, red is your color.* "I guess you like the sweater."

"I do and I should probably go get some more clothes. I know my wardrobe is woefully inadequate for this climate." Handing him a small box, she smiled. "I saved a few for you."

Without pause, he ripped the box open to find half a dozen neatly arranged *Brownies Picantes*. His mouth watered and he popped one in his mouth. The gentle layers of chocolate and cinnamon melted on his tongue as the pinch of ancho pepper finished it off.

"Trinity told me you liked them."

Without thinking, with the bite of the spicy chocolate still on his tongue, he kissed her. A slow, lingering kiss.

When he pulled away, a healthy blush of red covered her cheeks. "Guess you like the food."

"Yeah, I do." Kyle couldn't get over how every time he saw her, she was even more beautiful than before.

Almost no makeup, her hair slightly windblown, her deep brown eyes looking straight into his soul.

They stood in awkward silence until she pointed toward the kitchen. "Smells good. Can I help with anything?"

"Damn, I'm sorry. The brownies—"

"Right, the brownies. They do space people out sometimes." She ran her fingers along her lips as though she still felt his kiss.

"And thank you for bringing that to my crew today. They ate everything you brought." Popping another sweet back, he chewed, savoring the perfect flavors as they each blended on his tongue.

"I'm so glad. That's a lot of hard work you're doing up there. Much easier when you're not hungry."

"True." He pointed to his limited wine selection. "You

want to open a bottle?"

"Wine would be great." Her eyes went wide. "I'm impressed that you have two refrigerators."

"Gotta store the reds and whites differently."

"I'm surprised you know this."

"My mom's a wine snob. She taught us all this early."

"Sounds like your mom and I would get along."

He shook his head as he mumbled to himself, "No, you wouldn't."

"What?"

"Nothing. You like lemon chicken?"

"Yep." She joined him in the kitchen with a bottle of Pinot Grigio. "You have a lovely selection."

"Thanks." Dishing the chicken out on three plates, he tried to arrange it the way he'd seen it in restaurants.

Resting her hand on his shoulder, she asked sweetly, "Wine opener?"

He pointed to his right. "It's in the middle drawer."

"Thanks. This should complement…oh my." She stood at the far counter.

"What are you—"

"This is you?" She held up one of the calendar pictures.

Great. Just great. Nothing like having cover model pictures of yourself lying around. That doesn't scream I love myself at all. Swallowing hard, he nodded. "Yes."

An appealing wash of red colored her cheeks as she looked at the photo again. "You'll sell a million copies."

A relieved laugh escaped him. "We don't need to sell that many, but thank you."

Placing the photo back with the others, she pulled out the wine opener. "Why is your face hidden?"

I wish I could explain it. "Going for an international man of mystery theme."

Raising an eyebrow, she popped the cork on the bottle and smiled. "Yeah, baby. Yeah."

Her adorable attempt to mimic Austin Powers had him laughing. "Oh be-have."

The woman knows movie quotes. Should I get a ring now or tomorrow?

Within minutes, they'd taken their seats to enjoy his signature meal of lemon chicken, baked potatoes, and broccoli. The conversation flowed easily. They had similar tastes in movies, music, but Kyle's travel adventures were what appeared to get her attention the most.

"I'm jealous. Moving here was the first time I'd ever been out of Texas." She pushed a piece of broccoli around her plate before stabbing it with her fork. "That's why I took my time driving here. To take in more of the country."

"My parents encouraged me to travel as much as I could. Said it gave me a better perspective of the world." The rich flavor of the wine she'd selected perfectly mingled with the bite of the lemon pepper. "Where else did you stop other than Fort Collins?"

"Carlsbad Caverns, Roswell. I had to see the aliens museum." Her playful wink gave him an instant hard-on.

Standing to relieve pressure on his fly, he grabbed the bottle and topped off their glasses. "It's a weird place, but if you're close to it, you gotta see it. You went up 255 to 25, then?"

Her eyebrows popped up. "You know the roads, too?"

He chuckled at her surprise. "Done a lot of driving. That must have taken you up through Colorado Springs and Denver."

"We stayed in Denver overnight. I'd like to go back. There was plenty to do there. See a Rockies game." Her index finger slowly traced up the stem of the wineglass as she appeared lost in thought. "It would be fun to go spend a long weekend there."

His eyes watched her finger gently move up and down the stem. Instantly, his mouth went dry and he took a long swig of his wine hoping to quench his building thirst.

"Then we stopped in Fort Collins to visit...family." Without looking at him, she finished off half of her wine. "It was a nice visit."

His eyes darted from her eyes to her glass. "That good huh?"

At first, he worried he'd crossed the boundaries of first date etiquette, but when she giggled, he released a breath he didn't realize he'd been holding.

"I don't know what I expected, but it wasn't horrible, just not as productive as I'd hoped." She lifted a shoulder.

"It's what it is, I guess. Can't get people to change if they don't want to."

Leaning forward, he placed his hand over hers. "You mentioned it was Trinity's aunt you visited."

"Yes."

"Trinity said she was your adopted goddaughter?"

"Yes, my best friend, Laurie, was her mom."

"Was?"

Inhaling a long breath, Gabriella appeared to be mentally collecting the right words. "Laurie was my best friend growing up. She didn't have the greatest home life. Her parents fought a lot. They were never married so each of them figured they didn't have to stay if they didn't want to."

"Being married doesn't mean people stay either," Kyle answered before thinking.

Gabriella's lips thinned as she nodded. "True, but they used it to justify their absences."

"I see."

"She and her siblings were on their own quite a bit, especially when the parents were off doing their own things." She made lazy circles on the table with her finger. "Laurie hung out at my house as much as she could. My parents didn't mind the extra kids. They were all about family."

He rested his hand on her arm. "Sounds like your parents are good people."

"They are. Mom and Dad never turned any of our friends away." Tears suddenly began to fall. Gabriella quickly wiped them away. "Sorry, um, Laurie really tried to walk the straight and narrow. She got decent grades, but she wasn't life-focused at all."

"Sounds like my brother, Coleman." *Dammit, quit telling her family members' names.*

"Coleman. That's an interesting name. Trinity mentioned you had a sister. Artist, right?"

"Yes. That seems to be the only thing she can focus on, which is good because she's about to have a gallery showing." *Dammit.* The less they knew about him right now, the better.

"That's impressive."

"Yes." If he didn't get them off this topic soon, he'd have to come clean about who he was and he simply wasn't ready to go down that road. Especially if he was leaving. "But you were talking about Laurie?"

"Right. She graduated and enlisted in the army."

Kyle lifted a shoulder. "Sometimes military is a good way for people to get their heads on straight."

"She got through basic pretty well. Seemed to have found a groove. Within a year, she called me to tell me she was married and pregnant. He was in the military, too. She seemed to be happy. I was happy for her."

"Gabriella, you don't have to tell me any of this." He gently squeezed her shoulder.

She waved him off. "No, no, it's okay. When Trinity was born, Laurie called me, crying, because the baby didn't look *anything* like her husband."

"Who did Trinity look like?"

"According to Laurie, she looked like her husband's best friend."

That hit Kyle straight in the gut. "What did she want you to do?"

"She asked me to take care of Trinity because she wanted to make things work with her husband. He was fine raising his own child, but not his friend's."

Kyle's gut uncomfortably churned. "What happened?"

Holding her wineglass, Gabriella sighed. "She said she had nothing else to keep her on a good path except the military."

"Nothing else to keep her on a good path? She had a child."

"I know, but Laurie wasn't great at the reality of life sometimes."

"What about her family?"

Gabriella shrugged. "None of them were capable of caring well for themselves, much less a baby. Besides, they never liked Laurie's husband anyway. Now that they knew Trinity was biracial, they *really* didn't want anything to do with her."

Poor kid. "What about the bio father? Where did he fall in this?"

"She said that he was already in Special Forces training and a baby wasn't part of the plan."

"He dumped his kid for Special Forces? What a jerk."

Kyle took a few gulps of wine to keep himself from talking. He knew all too well what it was like to be dumped by a parent. When their own needs outweighed a child's.

Placing her hand on his arm, she shook her head. "Honestly, I can't trust that she even told him or that she even knew for sure who the bio dad was."

"I see." Shaking his head, he moved a piece of chicken around on his plate. "You took Trinity, then?"

"Of course. She was a baby. My goddaughter. She didn't ask for any of this."

I knew I liked this woman for a reason. "What did your parents say?"

"They didn't hesitate. Family is family. My mom and I drove up and got her. Trinity's been with us ever since."

"She never went back?"

"No, within a year, Laurie and her husband…died. Car accident. Head-on collision with another car."

Kyle's forehead furrowed. "Her family didn't step up?"

"They didn't fight for custody. In fact, Laurie made me her guardian as soon as Trinity came to live with us because she knew how her family felt about anyone who wasn't white."

"They were okay with you raising her, but not okay with raising her themselves."

She held her hand up. "They're selective bigots. They're fine if with you if you're not related to them, which seems ridiculous, I know. When Laurie called me and told me about Trinity, it wasn't a hard decision to take her in and then adopt. It's just that sometimes, like now, I begin to second-guess myself."

The worry in her voice concerned him. "I noticed she doesn't call you mom."

When she sniffed and more tears fell, Kyle mentally slapped himself.

You idiot! You're making her cry, again! "Damn, Gabriella, I'm so sorry."

She waved him off. "She did until we stopped and visited with her aunt a few days ago. I have no idea what happened and she's not telling me anything."

"I was a jerk to my mom too at that age." Kyle smirked before he took another sip of wine. "I made her life hell for a few years."

"Things better now?"

"I grew up. Realized you can't stay mad forever at people for being human. Screwing up." Although, he knew he'd never completely forgive his mother for the hell she put his dad through before he died. He cupped her face, wiping away her tears with his thumbs. "I didn't mean to make you cry."

"No, it's okay. I've need to blow off some steam. It's been a stressful week."

More tears ran over his hands. Gently, he wiped them away. "You keep blowing off steam like that and I'll need to get my mop out."

"I can think of better ways to decompress." Her eyes went wide. "Oh, that didn't come out right. I meant—"

He'd been a gentleman all evening, but seeing her lay her emotions on the table like that, he couldn't think of anything else to help her. Tasting her sweet lips was the only thing that came to mind.

Of course, it had been the only thing on his mind for the past hour. The past twenty-four hours.

A tender kiss, nothing more.

Simply something to take the edge off of his libido that had been this side of animalistic, but when he began to pull away, she pulled him flush against her.

Chapter Thirteen

WHEN HE TOUCHED her face, her panties damned near melted off. Then he kissed her and all bets were off.

Maybe it was the wine or the wide-eyed look of surprise when she let it slip about better ways to de-stress, but she didn't want to hold back any longer.

As he pulled away, she wrapped her arms around him and pulled him close until her lips brushed his.

"Kiss me," she whispered, not even sure if she should say it, but had no way of stopping herself.

"Yes, ma'am." His tongue tickled the inside of her lip before sweeping inside her mouth. He tasted of wine and pepper.

Gabriella greedily grabbed handfuls of his shirt as she soaked him in.

As he traced a line of kisses to her ear, the images of his calendar pictures raced through her mind. How the light danced across his chiseled body.

The tight, defined lines of muscles.

The pregnancy-inducing smirk.

Her heart beat faster at the realization of Mr. October

kissing her right now.

Any anger about her ex-fiancé's infidelities melted away.

He can have his pregnant girlfriend. I'll take my calendar man.

"Gabriella," he whispered. He brushed his hands along the sides of her body, making her nipples peak. She wanted to arch into his palm, feel his skin against her bare breast, feel his mouth on her. All of her.

Out of the corner of her eye, she spotted the card Trinity made to go along with the snacks they'd taken over earlier.

How sweet, he kept the card.

The tingle of his thumb grazing over her nipple yanked her sensible.

What are you doing?

"Gabriella?" He slowed his pace, gently pulling away, but keeping her close.

You've known him twenty-four hours. You have a daughter at home.

Still trying to gather her breath, she gave him a stressed smile while her rational brain fought with her irrational libido. "There's nothing more I'd like to do than take this further."

"But?" He moved a lock of hair out of her face. "You don't want to take things too far, too fast, right?"

No. I want to jump your bones right now. "Right. Yes."

A look of disappointment settled in his eyes, but he agreed. "Probably a good idea. Take it slow."

"Right. Yes." *I really hate being a responsible adult.*

He kissed her again, a slow, tender kiss before tilting his forehead to touch hers. "Maybe go out again in a few days?"

"You're working, I guess."

"Yep, at the station. Tomorrow." Sitting back, he held her hand. "I'll try and give you a call if it's slow, but who knows what it'll be like with the weather coming in tonight."

"I'll be at the diner if you need any food delivered." *That didn't sound clingy girlfriend-like at all.*

"I'll let the guys know, but I'm on kitchen duty. I've got it covered."

"What are you making?" She picked up her plate, helped him clear the table, and wrapped up the plate for Trinity, all while her body continued to hum.

"You're eating it. Lemon Pepper Chicken." Opening the refrigerator, he presented several bags of chicken.

A laugh escaped her. "When Flo said you only made lemon chicken, she wasn't kidding."

"Nope." He waved her off as she began to do the dishes. "Gabby. I can get this. Let me walk you home."

The winds whipped around them, knocking them into each other as they listened to the crunchy grass.

When they made it to her front door, she kissed his cheek. "Thank you for a wonderful evening. I haven't had a night out in a long time. It was delicious."

The corner of his mouth twitched as he chuckled. "Glad to do it. I'll see you very soon."

"Yes, you will." After closing the door and putting the

food away, Gabriella approached her daughter's room. Trinity sat on her bed, staring at her computer, her earbuds in. Curled up next to her, Cookie cat slept while Belle slept in the doorway.

"Hi. How's it going?" Gabriella leaned against the doorframe, careful not to step on the dog.

Without looking at her, the teen held up a thumb. "Have fun at Kyle's?"

"He made enough for all three of us. Brought you a plate. It's in the refrigerator."

That pulled her away from her screen. She pulled her earbuds out. "He made me food?"

"Yes, lemon chicken, baked potato, and broccoli. I think he thought we'd all come over."

"That's really nice of him to include me."

"Why wouldn't he? You're my family." Gabriella wondered how long it would take before Trinity called her mom again.

The teen shrugged. "True, but I see the way he looks at you, and I'm pretty sure he was glad to have you to himself for the evening."

Gabriella looked away as her cheeks warmed. His touch still lingered on her skin. "I won't lie. It's nice to have someone interested in me."

"You deserve someone who's nice to you. Someone who's got a good job. Isn't a jerk."

An unease sat in her gut at her daughter's too-nice responses. "You're right. I do." Motioning for Trinity to move over, she sat next to her. "What are you watching?"

"*Friends.*"

"Mind if I join you?"

As Trinity pulled the earbuds out, the sound of Ross asking what Chandler Bing's job was filled the room.

Trinity rested her head on her mother's shoulder as they settled in for an evening of lighthearted fun and laughter.

After two episodes, Gabby decided she'd head to bed. As she reached the doorway, Trinity sighed. "Gabby?"

"Yes, T."

"Can I ask you something?"

"Of course." She leaned against the doorframe.

"My aunt said I'm not respecting my mother by calling you mom." She cringed as she said the last words.

Biting her lip, Gabriella had to suppress the string of obscenities that could easily flow right now. *Not respecting Laurie? Ironic coming from people who wouldn't take in a child because of her skin color.*

But she wouldn't dump that on her daughter. "Trinity, I think your aunt still misses her sister. I'm sorry you feel like you've been put in a difficult place."

"I kinda do, but then again, you're the one who's been there for me all this time. Not her. Not Laurie."

Sitting back on the bed, Gabriella reached out and patted her child's hand. "Understand—your mom loved you enough to make sure you had a safe and nurturing place to be. She may not have been there for you, but she entrusted me to do that job because she knew I could do it well."

"I guess so, but there are times I wish she would have tried to keep me."

How she wanted to explain the ugly of it all to her, but what good would it do? "Know that I love you and would do anything for you."

"Really?"

More than you know. "All I want for you is to keep talking to me because I do want the very best for you."

"Thanks, Gabby."

Chapter Fourteen

"That's Judge McCorkle. He tends to hold court here frequently." As the morning rush began to wane, Flo pointed out regulars to Gabriella.

The thick smells of bacon, pancakes, and the cinnamon bread she'd introduced to the employees yesterday, drifted through the happy conversations. Pride swelled in her chest. Seeing the happy faces of her customers always blissed her out. She walked the room, topping off coffees, subtly replacing napkins, and removing empty plates.

Trinity, along with Miss Collier, Frederick, and an additional teen, sat in the corner. All looked like they were having a great conversation.

Please let them be good to her. Thinking about her daughter suffering the heartbreak of bullying planted a pain deep in Gabriella's chest.

Seeing the group talking and laughing gave her comfort that maybe this change might turn out all right.

When she placed the empty coffee pot back and started a new round, Flo continued, "The big man over there with the little boy, that's Colt Ewing and his stepson, Parker. They come in a lot and Parker likes chocolate sauce on his pancakes."

Another couple of smiling customers patted their bellies as they exited. It had been a chaotically busy morning and Gabriella took that as a good sign. Apparently, the locals weren't worried about her changing much or they were curious about the new owner.

Whatever the reason, Gabriella couldn't be happier with the day so far. "I'll make a note of that, but only chocolate sauce on pancakes? Not chocolate chip pancakes? No whipped cream? Sprinkles?"

"You know, I've never asked him." Flo thinned her bright pink lips. "Colt drives Parker to school because Talon, who used to work here, Parker's mom, drives to Bozeman each day for vet school."

"She must be very smart. Vet school is tough to get into."

"Yes. Colt comes in on Fridays after Parker has sports practice—not sure what he plays—and they get dinner to go."

Wiping down the counter, Gabriella switched out two half-full saltshakers with two full ones. "Do they get anything in particular?"

"Nope, Parker gets to pick so who knows what the kid wants. He probably doesn't even know until he comes in."

A warmth wrapped around Gabriella's heart as she watched Parker and Colt. The giant of a man obviously had a soft spot for his stepson. He helped him cut up his pancakes and made sure the youngster didn't spill his milk.

They come in for the food and stay for the conversation.

"Looks like a sweet family. Glad we can help their day go easier." Gabriella restocked the napkins as she made mental notes. "Talon come in at all?"

Prying Flo for information about the locals had been a godsend. With the exception of tourists, it seemed the woman knew everyone and everything any of them had ever eaten. "You getting all this or am I throwing too much at you at once?"

"Making sure I have this right. The Scott brothers are here on Wednesdays, the Wright sisters come in after their movie night, which can be any day of the week. The Ewing family comes in on Fridays to pick up dinner. Freddie comes in on Wednesdays because his mom works a double at the hospital."

"Exactly. See, you're getting the hang of it."

"Casey! Order up!" Merlin, the cook, yelled over several plates of food.

Casey held up her index finger as she took an order from a table of out-of-towners who appeared to be taking their time looking over the menu.

"I wonder if she needs me to run this order." Watching, Casey flashed a stressed smile at one of the women, who kept pointing back and forth to the two sides of the menu. Watching the second hand of her watch, Gabriella counted fifteen seconds. *Too long.* "I'm going to take this."

"I'll get the coffees covered."

Scooping up the plates, she delivered the meals, refilled their drinks, and cleared plates from another table.

Adrenaline coursed through her veins as she moved about the room, anticipating when customers needed something.

A clean fork to a woman who dropped hers.

A small stack of napkins to the couple with the toddler wrist-deep in pancakes.

Another refill on the judge's coffee as his booming voice hovered above the rest of the conversations.

Working the diner gave Gabriella purpose, joy to see everyone happy, fed, and satisfied.

A lovely redhead with blue eyes sat at the counter as a seat opened.

Gabriella quickly cleaned the area before the woman even put her purse on the counter. "Good morning. What can I get you?"

"I'll start with coffee." She extended her hand. "I'm Lucy, in case you forgot."

"I met you and your friend yesterday, right? Nice to meet you, again."

"Used to live here. Knew Harry and his family."

"You grew up in Marietta?" Sliding a coffee mug in front of her latest customer, Gabriella guessed that Lucy had to be about her age. Lucy talked about coming back and visiting friends including Keely Anderson.

Gabriella enjoyed the conversation with someone who knew the town as well as Flo did. "Sorry if I have to ask your name a few times. Still learning everybody. Your friend's name is Kelly?"

"Keely. She's great. Smart as a whip. Working on her doctorate in rocks."

"She sounds interesting. I look forward to seeing her, again."

"Great. She'll be here shortly. She has a weakness for Griffin's pancakes." She looked around Gabby. "Isn't that right, Griffin?"

"Yep." The cook nodded as he placed two more plates full of food in the window.

As Lucy and Gabriella talked, multiple customers came and went.

By the end of the shift, Gabriella had been properly updated on the most recent town gossip, learned that Lucy could put away the coffee by the gallon, and Keely could eat her weight in pancakes.

Casey handed over all her tickets. "Thanks for helping me back there. Those ladies couldn't decide if they wanted to be naughty and get something fried or stay with their wheat toast and cups of fruit."

"Glad to do it. How'd you do?"

Counting out her tips, Casey folded the bills in half and stuffed them in her pockets. "Wow. Busy morning. I could get used to this."

"So could I," a deep voice mumbled.

A shiver ran up Gabriella's spine as Kyle's words danced across her skin.

She turned to find him sitting at the counter. "Good morning."

"Got your boys' orders cooking, Kyle," Griffin yelled through the kitchen window.

"Thank you, sir." Kyle saluted before his eyes rested on her. The sultry stare made her feel all sorts of naked…and she liked it.

"What can I get—"

Casey pulled Gabriella's arm before she finished her sentence and took her to one side. "Hey, don't get your hopes up on that one."

"Oh?"

"I mean he was nice to show you guys around on that first day, but Kyle hasn't dated anyone since he's been in town. A real loner."

Seems she's been talking to Flo. "Thanks for the update."

"My brother, Brett, said Kyle doesn't do much except work and work out. I'm pretty sure he's taken a vow of chastity or he's got some super-secret past, like a spy or something."

Biting her lip, Gabriella suppressed the urge to contradict. "Thanks, Casey, I'll keep that in mind."

As she returned, the corner of his mouth mischievously

curled up. "Good morning, Miss Marcos. Who do I have to know to get some service around here?"

"I might know someone. What would you like?" Placing a coffee mug in front of him, she filled it.

He raised an eyebrow. "What do you have?"

Tingles danced along her body and settled between her thighs. "What are you hungry for?"

Right in the middle of the restaurant, he placed his hand on her wrist, pulled her forward, and kissed her before answering, "You."

"Oh."

It was as if the world was on pause. Almost everyone in the diner stopped moving and stared wide-eyed at them. With Kyle's back to the room, he didn't see a thing.

But Gabriella immediately felt all eyes on her. "Everyone's looking at us."

He gave her a quick kiss before sitting down and grabbing a menu. "Let them look."

"Is kissing outlawed in Marietta?"

A sly smirk spread across his face. "This isn't *Footloose*."

Lucy and Keely hummed the catchy movie song and gave her a thumbs-up before they shared a healthy slice of orange-glazed cinnamon bread.

Smoothing out her apron, Gabriella mumbled, "Am I missing something?"

Out of the corner of her eye, Casey stood with a pot of coffee in her hand, slack-jawed.

Casey's words of caution replayed in Gabriella's mind. "Oh, I see."

Flo rolled her eyes. "Come on, people, back to yourselves."

As if someone hit play, customers returned to their regularly scheduled programs.

Nestling the coffeepot, Casey fanned herself. "Wow. Nice job."

"Thank you." Heat spread across her face as she tried to subdue a nervous giggle.

Lucy leaned back in her chair and gave Kyle a once-over. "You're new in town?"

It took a second for him to notice Lucy had asked him a question. "Me? Been with the fire department about a year. Came in to pick something up."

"You knew Harry?"

A quick flicker of sadness drifted across his face. "I knew him. Good guy."

"The best." She dabbed the corner of her mouth with her napkin. "Sorry, but you look so familiar. I know I've seen you somewhere."

Without looking at her, he shook his head. "Don't think so."

"You sure?"

He slid his hand over to rest on Gabriella's. "Yes. I'm sure."

As endearing as the gesture was, his immediate rebuttal

hit her strangely. Before she could ask him anything, the sweetest word tickled her ears.

"Mom."

Mom? A tapping on the counter yanked Gabriella out of her bliss. "What?"

Trinity smiled at her. "Mom."

Mom. One word couldn't sound more melodious. She swallowed her joy to remain casual. "Yes, T? How's it going with Miss Collier?"

"She offered to take me to school today. With two other students, Tia and Frederick." A blush of red colored her cheeks when she mentioned the young man's name. "Freddie said they'd show me around. Eat lunch with me."

"Hello, Miss Marcos." The dark-haired young man extended his hand to shake. "Nice to see you again."

Returning the gesture, Gabriella smiled. "Frederick."

"And I'm his cousin, Tia." The chestnut-haired girl stepped forward. Her blue eyes were a beautiful compliment to her olive-colored skin. "I'm a freshman and Freddie's a sophomore. We'd love to show Trinity around. She's amazing."

Wringing her hands together, Trinity's eyes twinkled with excitement. "They said they're putting together an art display with the metal shop students. Said I could help since I know how to use basic tools."

Seeing the hope in her daughter's eyes caused excitement to lodge in Gabriella's chest. She had to clear her throat a few times before she could answer. "Yes, of course you can go with them, T. I've already done all the paperwork online. You should be registered, but please call me if I need to do anything else."

"If there's a problem, we'll just sign her in as a visitor today." Miss Collier handed over her ticket for the meal with two twenties. "High school's out at four-thirty. I'd be glad to bring her home or here."

Gabriella handed her money back. "No, no, this one's on me."

"You sure?"

"Please, let me do this. You have no idea how happy I am you came by. Oh, and I'll pick her up. Thank you for the offer." Pulling Trinity into her arms, she hugged her tight. "Have fun."

"Thanks, Mom."

Mom. Tears pricked the backs of her eyelids, but she kept them at bay.

With a skip in her step, Trinity walked out with her new classmates, giving her mom a wave before they exited.

"Thanks for the heads-up." Miss Collier patted Kyle on the shoulder before giving Gabriella a wink. "She's a smart girl. She's gonna be a great fit at Marietta High School."

As soon as the diner door closed, she tapped the counter in front of Kyle. "You did that?"

He lifted a shoulder. "I might have mentioned it when I saw Chelsea at the hardware store yesterday."

Leaning forward, she whispered, "You're gonna get so lucky for that."

Chapter Fifteen

*Y*OU CAN'T SLEEP *with her.*
The idea whipped around in his head like a flag in high winds.

All during his twenty-four-hour shift, he kept telling himself that, but neither his heart nor his cock would listen.

You're going to get so lucky. The way she'd said it had been so damned sexy that he wanted to pull her into her office and show her a proper Marietta welcome.

Once he arrived home, he noticed her house was dark. "Probably at the diner."

With the storm, they'd been plenty busy at the station going out to help with car accidents and people needing hospital transport.

Before he could even get out of his clothes, he flopped down on his bed and fell asleep.

Several hours later, his phone went off. Rubbing the sleep out of his eyes, he glanced at it. The name on the screen woke him straight up. "Dean?"

"You rang, Cavasos?" A deep voice asked.

"I need a favor."

"What is it?"

As Kyle explained the situation, his concern about the property decreased.

Dean had always been a good friend and a better listener. "You want me down there, when?"

"As soon as you can get there." Groggily, he made it to his desk and scanned the documents his mother sent him. The low hum of the scanner filled the room. "I'm going to send you the information. Tell me what the hell this is saying and if there's a way I can do what I suggested, because I don't know any of this crap."

"That's why you pay me the big bucks, right?"

As he tried to feed his photo shoot pictures into the scanner, he stopped and laughed at his fatigue. He tossed the photos on the same pile as the contracts. "I know you're busy, but I want to stay here. It's good people and away from all that shit."

"I hear ya. If anyone deserves a life of peace, it's you." Dean hummed one of Mumford & Sons' latest songs. "I can be down there by tomorrow. How long did you want me to stay?"

Relief spread through Kyle's shoulders. "As long as it takes to get the info I need."

"I'll read through these and get you an answer."

"Thanks, man. I knew I could count on you."

"But it'll cost you."

That made Kyle freeze in his tracks. "What do you

want?"

"What's her name?"

For the next hour, Kyle told his best friend everything.

"Her family works there? You want me to get intel on them too?"

"Not intel, but I think they'd be good resources." Although that idea didn't sit as well. "Just treat them right, okay? They sound like good people, good at their jobs and if Riley's screwing things up, I don't want to lose solid employees."

"I'll see what I can do. I'll let you know when I'm there. Talk to you then."

Lying back on his bed, Kyle rubbed his temples. Within minutes, he'd fallen back asleep.

With her schedule and him working over at Harry's House on Sunday, he didn't see Gabby until Monday when she came back home after taking Trinity to school.

Even though it had been less than two days since he'd seen her, his gut twisted like it had been years. As casually as he could muster, he walked over as she pulled into the driveway and handed her a cup of coffee. "Morning."

"Thank you." She gave him a quick kiss on the cheek. "How are you? It's been a bit."

"Good. Not working at the diner today?" His libido simmered below the surface.

"I have to be there later, but this morning, Flo has it handled."

"So if you're free this morning, I wondered if you'd like to do something."

"Yes." Her eyebrow cocked up. "What did you have in mind?"

Leaning in, he whispered, "Would you be interested in picking up where we left off the other night?"

The coffee mug stopped midway to her full lips. "You mean, alone time? Just us?"

"If that's what you want to call it." He stuffed his hands in his pockets as the chilly air did little to calm his lust.

At first, he thought she'd say no, but when she asked for a few minutes, he ran back home and brushed his teeth again.

When he heard her quick footsteps up his front stairs, Kyle couldn't open the door fast enough.

Without a word, he pulled her into his arms and kissed her without restraint.

She tasted like spearmint.

He smiled. "Cheater, you brushed your teeth."

"So did you." A slow smirk spread over her face as she ran her finger along his lower lip. "Your peppermint mouthwash makes my lips tingle."

"Maybe I could make other things tingle, too."

Her eyebrows hit her hairline. "Oh, my! That would be…um…um…"

"Yes, it would." He captured her mouth again as his mind raced with the things he wanted to do to her. How he wanted to touch her. Taste her. Bring her to climax and hear her scream his name.

He slid his hands down the gentle curves of her hips and back, pushing her sweater up. With tender strokes, he ran his thumbs along the sides of her breasts.

She moaned into his mouth before she pulled away and helped him remove her top layer.

"I've been dreaming about getting you out of that sweater for days." He growled as he tossed it across the room and marveled at her black lace tank top. His mouth watered at her perfect cleavage, the gorgeous swell of her breasts. "Did you want to take this somewhere else?"

"What?" Uncertainty flashed across her eyes.

"Or we could stand in the hallway if you want, but I think there are more comfortable places to sit."

"Sit. Sure." Her hesitation only intrigued him more. He'd dated enough wannabes to know when someone had ulterior motives. Gabriella's lack of confidence was a far cry from those who wanted sex for the sake of sex.

"How about the couch?"

Relief washed across her face. "Yes. Much nicer than standing."

Taking her hand, he led her to his sectional and let her choose where she wanted to sit.

She sat in the middle. Immediately, he joined her, kissing her neck and inhaling whatever that subtle vanilla scent was she used. "You smell like a cookie."

A giggle escaped her. "I should have, but I didn't bring anything and I'm not on the pill."

Disappointment momentarily slowed his momentum before he answered, "I don't have anything either, but—"

"Really?" She pulled back, her eyes wide with surprise. "A guy like you doesn't have a stock of protection hanging around?"

"What do you mean a guy like me?" He traced his finger along her collarbone as he relished the softness of her skin.

"Lookin' like you do, I can't imagine your dance card isn't full most of the time."

Shaking his head slowly, he leaned in and nibbled on the tender points at the base of her neck. "I don't dance with just anybody, Gabriella."

"Oh, I see." She relaxed under his touch. "Good to know."

"You can ask around. There's been no one in this town I've even asked out."

"Flo told me."

"She would know."

She froze. "I'm glad because lying is a deal breaker for me."

His conscience whispered, *Tell her who you are. Tell her what you're doing.*

Shaking it off, he agreed with her before perfectly placing kisses along the swell of her breasts.

She sighed and ran her fingers through his hair. "Oh,

my, that's, that's—"

"Yes, it is." He laid a path of kisses from her cleavage to her collarbone as his fingers gently pulled the strap of her bra and tank top off her shoulder. He brushed his lips along the curve of her shoulder to her ear. "What can I do for you?"

She swallowed hard. "For me?"

"Yes. For you. To you." Her shocked look made him wonder what raced through her brain. "Come on, Gabby. Tell me. What can I do for you?"

"You, you can let me, um, take your shirt off you."

"Whatever the lady wants." Leaning back against the cushions he put his hands behind his head giving her full access. He figured she'd sit by him, but when she stood, then straddled him, he thought he might lose it then and there.

With nervous fingers, she made quick work of the buttons.

As soon as she opened his shirt, lust replaced her uncertainty. "Oh, my." Placing her hands on his skin, she fanned out her fingers and let her fingertips trace along the lines of muscle. "Better than I'd hoped."

"Glad to meet your expectations," he murmured. His control hanging on by a thread. "A shirt for a shirt?"

She raised her arms over her head.

He moved his hands up her body, allowing his thumbs to graze over her bra-covered nipples. A soft sigh escaped her as he pulled the tank top off and threw it across the room.

Reaching around, she unhooked her bra and let it slowly

fall. "You're perfect." Tentatively, he relished the feel of her skin as his palms glided across her hips, to her waist, and brushed the sides of her sensitive skin.

She leaned forward, resting her hands on either side of his head. "You're pretty good, yourself."

Nibbling on the pulse point of her neck, Kyle worked his way to her ear and whispered, "Let me show you just how good this peppermint mouthwash is."

Not giving her time to answer, he kissed down between her breasts and around her nipple before taking the tender flesh into his mouth. His tongue ran around the pink of her breast before nibbling the tip.

"Wow, that's intense."

"You want me to stop?"

"Absolutely not."

He smiled against her skin before suckling her breast while caressing the other one, rolling the nipple between his fingers.

She arched her back and moaned as she rocked against him. "That feels so good."

His cock strained against his fly. He worried he'd pop before too long.

With a quick move he laid her on the couch and adjusted himself. She sat up and reached for his jeans, but he grabbed her wrists. "You first. Right now is all about you, Gabby."

"But want to touch you."

"You will, but…" He worked down her body. Licking the valley between her breasts. Feasting on each nipple before kissing her belly button. When he reached the top seam of her jeans, he ran his tongue along it. "Do you want me to stop?"

"No," she panted as she unzipped and pushed her pants off her hips. "No, please don't."

He smirked as he helped her remove only the jeans and placed his hands on her when she tried to expedite things with her red lacy underpants. "Patience, sweetheart."

Although, he didn't know how much longer he'd hold out. She'd had him twisted tight for too long.

"Now, where were we?" Kyle moved back up her body and kissed her. Her arms wrapped around him as he relished her naked skin next to his. Slowly, he worked down her body again, but moved past her panties.

He chuckled at the disappointed look she shot him. "Don't worry, sweetheart. I haven't skipped anything."

She moaned his name while he kissed the insides of her knees, her thighs, and over her panties. "Kyle, you're killing me."

Hooking his fingers under the sides of her underwear, he slid them off and marveled at her. How many times had he thought of her naked on his couch? In his house? On his bed?

Now, he marveled at his dreams come true. Her curves. Her scent. Her soft skin.

His mouth watered at the chance to taste her. With gentle brushes of his lips, he worked his way from the inside of her knee to her sensitive folds.

"You're beautiful," he whispered as his thumbs brushed the tender skin of her inner thighs.

Her hands rested on her stomach and she arched her back as he increased his pace.

Inch by torturous inch, he kissed her, inhaling her sweet scent as he moved closer the core of her sex.

She threaded her fingers through his hair as he flicked her swollen nub with his tongue, making her gasp.

"You like that?"

"Yes," she softly moaned.

Tracing the seam of her outer lips with his tongue, he heard her whimper. "You want more?"

"Yes. More."

"What about…this?" His tongue slid between her folds and he nibbled on her clit, relishing how she writhed with his touch.

She gasped, "Yes. More. Tingles. More tingles."

He took her into his mouth and tenderly sucked her sensitive nub. He ran his hand along the curve of her hip and up her body until he cupped her breast. His thumb grazed over her peaked nipple as he increased the pressure of his tongue on her clit.

Her breathing increased as her hips began to rock. "Oh, it tingles. Oh, my…so good."

"You like that?"

"Yes, eat me. Don't stop."

His tongue tickled her swollen clit before he tenderly sucked. Then he'd run his tongue along the seam of her before starting over again.

She writhed under his touch. Her reaction to him inched him to the edge of his own climax.

He'd imagined getting to taste her, but hearing her tell him what she wanted only turned him on more. Reaching down, he popped the button and unzipped his jeans to release the pressure and give him more time with her.

Her eyes went wide with lust. She sat up. "I want to see you. All of you."

"But I'm not done with you yet."

"We'll take turns." She threaded her fingers through his belt loops and pulled him to stand in front of her. "I've dreamed of stripping you down."

"That's me, the dream maker." He let her slide his jeans off until they pooled to the floor. Before he could step out of them, he felt the warmth and the soft pressure of her mouth around his cock.

A moan escaped him as she tenderly sucked and slowly moved up and down. "Gabriella, damn, that's…yes. Feels good."

She ran her hand up his inner thigh before brushing over his balls.

She'd pull back to the head of his cock before taking him

back into her mouth and sucking again. Her hands wandered, cupping his butt, brushing against his chest, caressing his thighs, inching him to closer to losing it.

Her tongue traced along the rim of the head before she slid him between her lips again.

Up and down in torturously slow movements.

"Damn, Gabby. Yes. I. Good. So good." No rational thought existed in his brain but she shoved him to the edge when she cupped his butt and pushed him deep inside her mouth. He pulled away.

"Did I hurt you?" she asked.

"No." He pressed his lips to hers. "It's my turn."

Kyle marveled at her naked body. She had all the curves of a gently winding road and he planned to go on one long road trip.

He scanned her from the top of her head to her toes before leaning down and taking a nipple into his mouth.

She gasped as he applied a bit more suction this time while tracing along the seam of her with his finger and sliding it between her folds. Her back arched as she ran her fingers through his hair. "Oh! Yes."

Kissing her down her stomach, he didn't hesitate this time when he reached her sensitive nub. With his finger moving in and out of her, he feasted.

"Kyle, oh, yes, that, is a-a-a-mazing. Yes!" Her ragged breathing increased as she grabbed the sides of the couch.

Kissing her inner thigh, he growled, "You're so tight. So

close."

"Yes. Please, Kyle. Don't stop."

"Cum for me, Gabby." He slid another finger inside her and placed his thumb on her clit, wiggling it before nibbling her again.

"Yes. Yes. Yes. Kyle! Yes!" Within seconds, her inner walls clamped down on his fingers as she rode his hand.

Chapter Sixteen

A WEEK HAD come and gone and, according to Gabriella, Trinity had settled in well to her new life.

"The locals have really welcomed us with open arms," she sighed as she relaxed into the cushions. "But you're the only one who's welcomed me like that."

"Glad to be part of the welcoming committee." He kissed her inner thigh as bright rays of afternoon sun sparkled across Copper Mountain.

Gabriella panted as she laid back on the futon. "You're right, the view from here is beautiful."

Kyle smirked as he crawled up her body, his eyes raking over her perfect curves. "It really is. I could look at this view aaaaallll day." *And for the rest of my life.*

Giggling, she playfully slapped his arm. "Animal."

"Only around you." He growled and nibbled her earlobe.

She sighed as he ran his tongue down the curve of her neck. "Goodness, the tingles! How I love peppermint mouthwash."

It had been seven glorious days since that first fantastic morning with Gabriella and happily, they'd shared quite a few more *dates* since.

With Trinity in school during the day, they'd had a few alone hours here and there when the diner's afternoon lull kicked in and he had the day off.

Hanging out together in the evenings when he wasn't at the station or helping at Harry's House had become routine. Kyle helped Trinity with her science homework and she'd helped him learn to draw something other than stick figures.

Avoiding his own relatives for so long, he'd all but forgotten the comfort and warmth of family. The unexpected laughter, the dinners together, the mundane moments that were made special because of the other people in the room.

Who would have thought he could have found his happy ending in a town like Marietta, Montana?

Just thinking about the woman next to him made his body hum. Of course, it helped that Gabriella wore nothing but a tank top and her panties…no wait.

He'd stripped her of those and tossed them somewhere in the room after the minx surprised him with a mint of her own.

After she'd pushed him down on the futon and made quick work of his jeans, she'd popped a couple of mini Altoids from a tin in her jeans pocket right before she'd taken him into her sweet mouth. He didn't think he'd ever climaxed that fast in his life.

Then he returned the favor. Just thinking about tasting her again got him hard.

They'd yet to make it to his or her bedroom for an *official* date, but they'd had a helluva lot of fun with foreplay. He hadn't blamed Gabriella for not wanting to take that step, but it had become more difficult not to want to make love to her. Still, he had no doubt she'd be worth waiting for.

The blissful look on her face made him ask, "What are you thinking?"

"Thinking about how quickly things change."

He pulled her into his arms and she rested her head on his chest. Her soft hair fanned out over his shoulder as she ran her hand up and down his arm.

The early spring winds blew softly against the windows. He looked forward to the less chilly weather so he could take Gabriella and Trinity into the mountains, show them a close to bird's eye view of Marietta.

"I'd forgotten you were in the military." She motioned to the shadow box. "UCLA, huh? Your family live in California?"

He froze.

Immediately, she turned to face him. "You okay?"

His heart leapt to his throat, but he managed to squeak out, "My mother and most of my brothers and sisters are still there."

"Your dad not around?"

Depends on who you ask. "No. He's not."

"Was that a bad question?"

"It's fine." Letting his fingers walk down her back, he

watched her eyes close and the corners of her mouth twitch.

"Mmmmm, that feels good."

"It's supposed to." As his fingers approached the base of her spine, he flattened his hand and ran it over her luscious backside.

She let out a long, satisfied exhalation. "Kyle?"

"Yes, Gabriella."

"Why don't you want to answer questions about your family?"

The honest question sideswiped him. Jerking his hand away from her glorious ass, he gave her a friendly pat on the shoulder as rational excuses flip-flopped over in his mind. "I dunno. Not much to say. We're kind of boring."

Her eyes slowly opened. "Everyone thinks their family is boring or weird or crazy or whatever."

Or scandalous. "True."

"Okay, your family is boring. What about you?"

"What do you mean?"

"After living in Southern California and serving in the military, after all that, how in the world did you end up in a town like Marietta?"

For a moment, he didn't say anything. The words wouldn't come. He'd never spoken about Patrick with anyone other than his family.

"Kyle?"

The sweetness of her voice brought down his angst. He began draw lazy circles on her naked shoulder. "My dad,

Patrick, was the one who brought me to Marietta years ago. Ski trip. Just the guys."

Gabriella propped herself up on her elbow as her tank top shifted, giving him a perfect view of her cleavage.

His mouth watered at the potential of another go-round.

A slow smirk spread across her face. "Eyes up here, Kyle."

"Sorry." *Not really.*

"You've mentioned him several times. That's where you learned to fix all the stuff for Harry's House?" Subtly, she pointed. "Is that him? With you?"

Across the room, the photo of Kyle and Patrick sat on the side table near the treadmill.

Sadness lodged in his throat, but he swallowed it down. He wouldn't go there. "Dad made sure I could fix anything. Said it was better to know than to be a dumbass about it. Pay someone for a job I could easily do myself."

"Seems like good advice. My mom and dad taught all of us the basics. Tools. Home repairs. How to know when someone was trying to sell you something that you didn't need. I learned a lot listening to them and my grandparents." She flipped her hair out of her face. "I know it sounds very stereotypical, Mexicans being able to use tools, fix things, but it's a seriously underappreciated skill."

Without thinking, he rested his hand on her bare hip. "Agreed. People need to quit thinking that basic life skills are something you farm out. Not everyone out there does a good or honest job."

Nodding, she snuggled in again. "My grandfather wasn't a big fan of the girls learning such things, but my dad disagreed. He said his girls were going to be independent and not have to rely on a man to help them through life."

"Your dad sounds like a good guy."

"He is. Still tries to do everything even with his back all messed up."

"How did that happen?"

She shrugged. "He fell off a ladder during a job. He's mobile, but his endurance isn't what it used to be. Where did Patrick learn his skills?"

His heart beat a little faster for her innocent want for information. "My great-grandfather taught my grandfather and so on. Then my dad taught me."

"My grandmother let me help in the kitchen when my mom was watching the other kids. No one else seemed to be as interested in cooking or baking as I was." She sighed as he ran his fingers through her hair. "Those teaching moments are special. Unforgettable. I hope Trinity has a few with me."

"I know it's hard with a teenager. I gave my mom lots of grief at that age." *For a damned good reason, though.* He shook off that frustration. "It looks like Trinity has settled in."

"For now. I hope it sticks, but she was so unhappy in Lone Star Crossing." She smiled against his bare skin. "I know it's all normal, the teenage angst, but there are times I wish she were more like me and less like...her mom."

The pain in her voice hurt his heart. "She's a lot like you."

"Really, how so?"

"She's smart. Driven. Intelligent."

"Flatterer. You just want to get lucky again."

Cupping her butt, he growled, "That is true."

As he tried to kiss her, she placed her fingers on his lips. "Kyle, you do this when I ask anything about your family."

His libido quelled for a moment. *Tell her everything.*

"Sweetie." Her sweet voice momentarily calmed his angst. "Kyle?"

After taking a deep breath, he let it out and the words flowed. "My dad died when I was about twenty-three. Right after I'd finished my biology degree. He made it to the graduation ceremony, even though he looked like hell. Died a couple of days later."

"Was it sudden?"

"No, he'd been diagnosed with chronic myelogenous leukemia a few years before. Had a bone marrow transplant."

"You matched?"

"No, my sister did. The procedure just gave him more time." *And broke his heart.*

"I'm so sorry you lost your father. The way you've spoken of him, he sounds like a good man." The warm wet of tears caught him off guard and only made him like her more.

Glancing down, he asked, "Are you crying?"

Gabriella's full lips tilted. "A bit."

"Why?"

"You obviously miss your dad. I can hear it in your voice."

The sweet words hit him like a freight train. No one had ever said that to him before, then again, no one had ever taken the time to get to know him like she had.

Come on, Dean. Find me a way. "When I'm working on Harry's House, I think how he'd love to be here, helping me, getting things ready sooner. Better. I know he would."

His voiced cracked. He didn't really know anything because after his father found out Kyle wasn't biologically his, Patrick never looked at him the same way.

"Your mom still around?"

"Yes. She's alive and well." *Making my life more complicated by the minute.*

"I appreciate you sharing all that with me."

"You're welcome. Thanks for asking." There was so much more he could tell her. He wanted to. He wanted to tell her the entire, frustrating tale. As the words bounced around in his head, threatening to pop out of his mouth, he hugged her tightly.

She smiled against his skin. "Kyle, I want you to know that whatever you tell me, about your family or your life, stays between us."

Immediately, he loosened the hug, as if he'd kept her too close. "Why would you say that?"

Sitting up, she lifted a shoulder. "Because whenever I ask you anything about your family, you get very quiet, almost as though you're afraid to tell me something."

"That obvious, huh?"

"Look, I'm having a lot of fun with you, but I want to get to learn about you, too." Her tears welled up at the last few words. "I like you, *a lot.*"

"I sure as hell like you too, Gabby." *More than I should.* For years, he'd kept women at an emotional distance, especially those who'd known about his Hollywood pedigree. Without so much as a wink, Gabriella had burrowed under his skin and he hadn't even given up a fight.

Tell her, tell her everything. "Gabby, I—"

"Is that the time?" She sat up and looked at her watch. "Oh goodness, Trinity's out of school in fifteen minutes and I have to go back to the diner."

Disappointment settled in his gut. No matter how much he wanted it to stay still, life would keep moving forward. "I'll head to Harry's House and get a few things done."

"Did you want to come by for dinner?"

"I'd like that. Seven?"

"Sounds great." She stood and turned in a circle. "Where did you throw my bra? My panties?"

Replaying the moment he had her out of those damned contraptions, he shrugged. "Try the hallway."

"Animal."

Chapter Seventeen

THE CREAK OF the floor upstairs signaled that Trinity had finally rolled out of bed.

"Finally, we can get on the road." Gabriella had already made a morning trip to Monroe grocery store. Seeing small bottles of vanilla for three dollars and five-pounds bags of sugar for twice what she'd paid back in Texas still alarmed her.

Their move so far had been good. The diner's daily traffic had picked up a bit, profits were steady, but like any business, you had to plan for the worst and hope for the best.

Phone conversations with Angelica and family happened at least a few times a week.

Continued worry bubbled since Gabriella couldn't be sure if Riley Fitzgerald would keep his word about her family members' jobs.

It hurt knowing she'd kept them in the dark. She'd always been honest with her mother, but this time, Gabriella simply couldn't risk them losing everything they'd worked so hard for.

Since they'd arrived two weeks ago, last night had been

the first night it didn't freeze, but the temperatures still remained far colder than they were used to.

The steady drip-drip-drip of the melting snow softly tapped against her window.

Knowing the roads were clear, Gabriella had full confidence she could make the less than one-hour drive to Bozeman without problems.

These two glorious weeks had been all about learning what her customers did and didn't like, who the regulars were, and connecting with the local farmers and ranchers.

Trinity's life had vastly improved. She not only found a nice group of kids, but she thrived in her new school as well.

The beep from her phone interrupted the silence of the morning. The text bubble posted, "Drive safe. See you tonight."

Kyle.

She quickly returned with: "I will. You still want me to stop at Victoria's Secret?"

Last night she'd pulled up the map of Gallatin Valley Mall. The popular lingerie store certainly piqued his interest.

Giggling as his text bubble popped up, she anxiously waited for his response.

He'd been a constant in her life since she arrived. Life had been far richer, far more delicious with him in it.

Each time they'd talk, he'd reveal a bit more about himself. His parents' names; he had three sisters and a brother. He'd served in the Navy. Earned a biology degree. Where he'd traveled and how he now planned to stay in Marietta.

An entire line of throwing kisses emojis popped up.

Smiles. Hearts. Love.

Love?

Her heart slammed into her ribs.

Love.

With nervous fingers she sent back a smiley face emoji before dropping the phone on the table like a hot rock.

When she packed up her life to bring it to Marietta, the only things she had on her agenda were working and giving her daughter a better life.

Nowhere on her to-do list did she write "get involved with a super-hot, smart neighbor, spend a lot of naked time with said neighbor, and have the best foreplay ever."

Falling in love with him hadn't even entered her mind, but without trying, Kyle had become a necessary part of her world. Being without him simply hurt her heart.

Love.

Laughing at herself, she shrugged at how quickly life can change. "Ugh, Gabby. You've got it bad."

Rubbing the sleep out of her eyes, Trinity shuffled in, wearing her unicorn slippers and pajamas. "Morning."

"Sleep well?"

She mumbled something that resembled "yes" before grabbing a bowl, spoon, and a box of raisin bran. "What's on the agenda today?"

"It didn't freeze last night so we're good to go to Bozeman."

Trinity's eyes went wide. She practically threw the cereal back in the pantry and snatched a protein bar. "I'll be ready in ten minutes."

As Trinity got ready, Gabriella looked over their finances again. Sitting on the laptop computer on the table she set her last paycheck next to her. It arrived yesterday in the mail along with the copy of the non-disclosure and non-competition agreement that Riley insisted she sign.

The famous Winston Enterprises Logo was stamped on the back of both the unopened envelopes.

"Ugh, I'll deal with these later." Staring at the return address, she picked it up, but dropped it again, disgusted. "If only I could have talked to the owners. Certainly, they would have done something about him."

Still, she wouldn't balk at her last paycheck. She'd earned that and had at least got a bit of a retirement fund going in her years there.

With the diner doing well and them heading into the summer season, Gabriella had every confidence they would be more than financially comfortable as long as they didn't get crazy.

This had to work. *If I go back and don't work there again, I'm going to have to tell my family everything. Then all hell will break loose.*

Before leaving, they let Belle out, dried her feet, gave her a treat, and checked Cookie. She sent Kyle a quick text before backing out of the driveway.

On the list today were visits to Costco, Michaels Arts

and Craft Store, Target, and a mall with multiple stores they could check. With the end-of-winter sales, they could snatch up a few more much-needed warmer clothes.

The red sweater Kyle had given her had been a staple and always a wonderful reminder of how good it felt when he'd rip it off her.

She never thought she'd recover from his full lips on her body and he brought her to climax faster than any guy she'd ever been with. Not that there'd been that many before him, but still.

"We're going to the craft store, right?" Trinity's finger sailed across her screen. "Tia wondered if we could pick up a few things for her. She's short on these cool colored pencils and some sketch pads."

"We could do that."

Rich blues of the cloudless sky spread out in front of them as they drove 89 and away from town for the first time since they'd arrived.

Trinity drummed her fingers on her thigh as she stared at her phone. "Tia just asked if I can stay at her house tomorrow."

"That sounds like fun." Her heart fluttered at the idea of having a sleepover of her own.

As her daughter texted her friend back, butterflies danced around Gabriella's belly at the idea of taking the situation with Kyle a step further.

Victoria's Secret. Here I come.

Chapter Eighteen

THE MORNING AT the fire station had been interesting. No sooner had Kyle put his stuff in his locker, than they were called out to a car accident. A van full of tired tourists on their way to Copper Mountain from Northern California for a few days of skiing.

They'd skidded off the road when the driver had fallen asleep.

As soon as the injured were bandaged up, Kyle lectured the driver about driving when exhausted.

Deputy Logan Tate arrived as the tow truck pulled up. He gave them a ride into town right as another call came in.

This time, Eliza and Marshall McKenzie, the owners of the Bramble House Bed and Breakfast, reported something interesting.

A young, confused adult male elk had been wandering around the backyard, causing all sorts of destruction.

The houseguests as well as Eliza's great-aunt and longtime Marietta resident, Mable Bell, watched through the back kitchen window. The usually curmudgeonly woman had a slight smirk on her face as the first responders waved their arms in the air and yelled at the animal. It took about ten minutes before the men were breathless after running around in circles—wearing heavy boots and coats in almost knee-deep snow.

About the time they had run out of options, Brett Adams and Duke arrived.

Duke took one look at the elk and the dog's ears formed sharp points. Immediately, Duke put on his game face and off he went. Barking and wagging his tail, within two minutes he'd successfully herded the animal to trot along the stone wall that ran the length of the back of the property before the elk jumped a woodpile, kicking half of it over with his hind legs.

Finally, the dog *encouraged* the visitor out the back gate and down toward an embankment.

They watched the elk slosh along the banks of the Marietta River, making his way back toward the mountain range.

Duke went to each of the responders for a congratulatory high five as it were. As he slowly passed each member of the team, they'd reach out and scratch him behind the ears as they praised him.

He ended with Brett who gave the dog a large Milk-Bone dog treat.

On the way back to the firehouse, Kyle sat next to the open window of the truck and let the Montana air slap him in the face. Damn, he loved the crisp smell of the mountain air.

How the town looked when the first hints of spring began.

The life he'd made here had been a much-needed reprieve from his family's scandalous past. Marietta healed his wounded soul.

And maybe, just maybe, here he'd find peace.

And love.

They passed the familiar two houses on Bramble Lane, making him smile.

Shaking off the ideas of happily ever after, he simply focused on how good Gabriella had felt in his arms yesterday and so many days before.

She sure is someone I could get used to. More than get used to.

Dean had been more than helpful and verified what Kyle had feared. The combination of Riley's lack of business sense and his caustic personality was losing business. Plus, Preston hanging out at the resort and throwing parties until all hours of the night weren't sitting well with *paying* guests.

After last night's update and a quick discussion of the requirements of Kyle grandfather's will, he instructed Kyle to change a few things in the contracts. Write them in the margins, scan them in, and send the hard copies back to his mother to sign off on.

Hopefully the changes would appease everyone, but he couldn't be sure. No one had ever done what he was about to suggest with his grandfather's property, but for him to stay here, he had to do something drastic.

It had been almost four days since he'd Priority mailed it. He'd heard nothing from his mother. This could mean she'd received the papers and was deciding her next move or she'd given up.

And Lillian Winston-Cavasos hadn't given up on anything in her life.

Until he heard from her, he wouldn't worry about it.

He smirked at his mental brush-off.

He wouldn't worry about it *much*. His mother had a way of making things go her way, but Kyle planned to do everything he could to deflect her attempts to get him out of Marietta.

Especially now. Especially after Gabriella.

Even her daughter had grown on him. Kyle and she shared a similar sense of humor, a love for books, and the girl had patiently taught him how to draw something other than crappy stick figures.

Plus, he liked the instant dad role, like they were a family.

His family. *My family.*

That warmed his heart better than any coat he'd ever worn.

"Hey, Cavasos!" Brett yelled as soon as the truck stopped in front of the station.

"What, Adams?"

"Aren't you on cooking duty?" A wide smirk split his face

as he patted his belly. "It's after lunchtime."

"I've got it covered." Hopping out of the truck, Kyle ran up the stairs two at a time to shower up before the rest of the crew.

By the time the truck had been backed into the bay and the equipment unloaded, Kyle already had the chicken in the pan and had started on the sides.

The part-time firehouse dog, Brontë, sat at his feet while he worked.

Logan Tate wandered in and leaned against the counter. Brontë sniffed his shoes and wagged his tail. "How's it going?"

"Good. You?"

"Came by to talk to Jonah about someone they saw in the mountains."

"How old?"

"Not sure. Could be an adult or a teen."

The idea of Trinity being caught in that environment knotted up the muscles in Kyle's shoulders. "What do we need to do?"

"I'll go over it with Jonah first. He thinks it might be an adult hiker, but Keely's convinced it's a kid."

"Whatever you need, man. Glad to help." Stirring the rice after he poured it into the boiling water, Kyle squeezed in a bit of lime juice and dropped in a handful of herbs.

"We appreciate that, Kyle. Hey, sorry for taking off on you like that during restoration day. I had to take care of something."

Kyle bit his lip to keep from laughing. The something Logan had to take care of was making sure his lover, Charlie, didn't leave town. By-the-book Logan even hot-wired a patrol car to flag down the bus that Charlie was on to keep her from getting away from him. "No problem. Things better?"

Logan scooped up the dog, who tried to lick his face. "Helluva lot better."

"Those kids we helped out of the ditch okay?"

"Yep, dropped them off at the Graff. They're gonna get some sleep before heading to Copper Mountain. Their car should be fixed by tomorrow."

Sprinkling some cumin, cinnamon, and fresh cilantro over the chicken, Kyle grabbed a spatula. "Charlie's good?"

"She's great. I'm gonna marry that woman."

Marry. That punched Kyle in the gut. "Good for you."

With a chuckle, Logan pointed as Brontë leaned in for a better look. "That's some mighty fancy chicken you're making there."

Lifting a shoulder, he moved the food around in the skillet. "Gabriella suggested I try to branch out from lemon pepper and salt."

"No more of your signature dish?"

"Not today." Kyle focused on the recipe and tried not to think of the dark-haired chef naked.

"Glad to see you happy, friend."

Multiple footsteps signaled a few of the guys were done cleaning up.

"Staying for lunch, Logan?" Jonah called out.

"Don't mind if I do. I'll get the table ready." He put the dog down and washed his hands.

Thirty minutes later, the entire crew sat around the table feasting on Kyle's new recipe of spicy chicken, broccoli, and brown rice.

"This is good, Cavasos. What did you put in the rice?" Brett asked before shoveling more into his mouth.

Duke sat at Brett's side as Brontë sat next to Lyle Tate's chair. Both dogs certainly hoping that gravity would work in their favor.

"Cilantro and lime juice. Gabriella said it would mix things up a little." When he looked up, all eyes focused on him. "What?"

The corner of Lyle's mouth curled up in a mischievous grin. "You taking cooking tips, now?"

"Yeah, so? She owns the diner. Why wouldn't I take her advice?"

"Fair enough."

For the rest of the meal, the conversations stayed light and no one brought up the subject of the new girl in town.

Kyle mentally laughed at his protectiveness of anyone talking about Gabriella. *Now I understand why Jonah lost his shit that day.*

As if he could read his mind, Jonah gave Kyle a respectful

nod.

Instead, discussions finally changed to the upcoming calendar release.

Todd Harris elbowed the guy next to him. "You held out long enough, Jonah."

With his full fork halfway to his mouth, Jonah snarled, "Yeah, I did. Thanks for the stripper music during my photo session, Cavasos."

"Ah, come on, Jonah. Who doesn't like Def Leppard?" Kyle smirked at the ribbing they'd given the pilot since he'd held out to be the last of the group to pose.

"Then you had to up things by posing with a puppy," Logan laughed. "What you trying to be calendar model of the year?"

"Blame your girlfriend for that one, Tate," Jonah pointed at the broccoli and Todd handed him the bowl.

"Charlie does know what works. She said preorders are through the roof."

Kyle leaned back in his chair, appreciating the brotherhood the group had. "At least it's done. Now we can get that behind us and focus on finishing restoration."

"What's left to do?" Brett asked after scooping up a second helping of chicken.

"The wiring's done and I changed out the panel. The building inspector passed us on that. I've tried to get over there a few times a week doing something."

"Appreciate that, Kyle." Jonah nodded as he finished off

the rice and broccoli. "Didn't you get something done last week, Tate?"

"A few of us got walls painted upstairs." Lyle cut off a piece of chicken and dropped it on the floor. Brontë ate it before Duke had a chance to notice. "Emily, Charlie's sister, helped out."

"I heard." Logan lifted an eyebrow at his brother.

"I'm surprised you have time to do any of the restoration, Cavasos, with you at the diner so much." Brett smirked. "And her house."

"Knock it off, Adams." Logan threw his napkin at Brett's face. "Everyone's entitled to a private life. What else is there to do?"

Reining in his annoyance, Kyle continued, "Strip and restain the cabinets and put on new hardware. Knock out part of the kitchen wall to put in an island for the kids to sit around. The insulation has to go in."

"I can get that done." Brett cut off a piece of chicken and handed it to Duke, who waited patiently at his side. "What rating are we needing?"

The offer surprised Kyle, but he'd take the help. "For the attic, R49 to sixty. The upstairs floors, R25 to thirty. We've got the supplies. I'd like to make sure we're as efficient as we can get."

All the men nodded.

As Kyle went over the repairs in his mind and how he'd talked to the city about fixing the drainage issues, it reminded him of his father and how he'd go over everything before starting a new project.

What he wouldn't give to have his dad here. *He'd have that place up and running in no time and we'd have made amends somehow.*

"Sounds like a helluva lot of work. Think we'll meet our deadline?" Jonah asked before shoving another bite in his mouth.

Kyle shrugged, trying to calculate the timeline to opening. They had a good five weeks left, but if it snowed again, it would delay things. "The ground needs to thaw so we can dig and get the foundation issues repaired. Divert the water to drain away from the house and the ones surrounding it, but I've already talked to a couple of guys who are ready to go. Their designs work well for drainage issues."

"What about inside?"

"The heavy stuff is almost done. The rest is time-consuming, but we can pull in more people for the details."

Jonah, Lyle, Logan, and Todd all offered their significant others to pitch in as well as asking the guys from the Bake-Off to help.

Even Brett gave a thumbs-up and said he'd ask his sister to donate some of her time.

Thankful for the offers, Kyle breathed a sigh of relief. "If we can get a few good weekends of work in, we should be pretty well caught up and be ready in plenty of time."

His phone buzzed. Before he answered it, he saw three

missed calls from his mother, but seeing Gabriella's name, he greedily answered it. "Hey! Having fun on your shopping trip?"

"Yes, it's quite exciting here in the big metropolis of Bozeman," she said with a sigh. "Walking around Michaels while Trinity fills the cart with art supplies."

"Is that Gabriella?" Logan yelled. "Tell her thank you for teaching you to make something than Lemon Pepper Chicken."

The rest of the guys cheered.

"I heard that. You're welcome, guys."

Her voice always put Kyle in a good mood. "What's up?"

"We have a few more stops to make and should be home within the next couple of hours."

"I'll be here at the station if you need anything." He began to pick up his plate, but Brett grabbed it and gave him a respectful nod before taking them to the sink.

"How busy has it been?"

He moved to the other room and sunk down on his bunk. "Not bad. Steady. We had to help an elk."

"Did you say elk? Like moose?"

"Yes."

"Interesting. I have a big favor to ask."

The phone beeped. Kyle held it out to see his mother was trying to call again. He ignored it. "What can I do for you?"

"Can you go check on Belle really quick? We've got a few

more stops before we get on the road. We're staying out longer than I planned."

"Of course. Be safe."

"We will. You're a lifesaver, Kyle."

He moved away from the guys. "Did you get anything, um, *interesting?*"

"Maybe."

"Remember, make it easy to take off because it's not going to be on you that long." He shifted his weight, hoping to keep himself from tenting his pants.

She laughed. "Trinity's staying at Tia's tomorrow night. Maybe you'll get to see it for yourself then."

A night. By themselves? His fly almost popped the stitching. "Um, okay. Hurry back."

"See you shortly," she replied sweetly before hanging up.

When Kyle returned to the kitchen, Jonah looked right at him and said, "Man, you've got it bad."

Kyle had to laugh at the irony. "Gabby needed me to check on the dog real quick."

"Go ahead. I'll cover you."

Throwing on his jacket, Kyle asked, "Thanks man. Keely doing okay?"

"Yeah, thanks for taking care of her." Blowing out a long breath, the pilot's shoulders slouched. "I keep thinking about if she'd fallen farther than she did. What would I have—"

"But she didn't and she's okay." Extending his hand, the men shook. "You and I know what it's like to lose people.

Military threw us both in that shit, but we take the good stuff and don't question it."

"Right. Thanks, man. Go check on that dog."

In the short drive to her house, his happiness bubbled in his gut. He hadn't been this thrilled with life in years.

Simply walking through her house gave him a sense of calm. Peace.

What he wouldn't give to keep this going forever.

Belle danced around at the back door as soon as he entered. They wandered through the small yard as she took her time finding the perfect spot. After a few minutes, he got her back inside and dried her paws.

Cookie jumped on the kitchen table next to him, knocking over a stack of mail in the process, sending letters in all directions. "Come on, cat."

Picking up the envelopes, his heart leapt to his throat when he saw the familiar logo on the back of two of them.

"Winston Enterprises?" Even though he'd long figured out where she worked, his mouth went dry all the same. He held it up to the light and as best he could tell, one had to be a paycheck stub, the other, a letter.

The postal stamp read Lone Star Crossing, Texas.

Winston Enterprises.

Winston Resort.

Jewel of the Hill Country. Lone Star Crossing. San Antonio.

Belle gave him a curious stare before plopping down next to the floor vent.

Remembering the picture, he walked into the living room and looked at it again. The edges of that familiar sign poked out behind a couple of her family members.

"I hope this works." Rubbing the bridge of his nose, he collected his thoughts. "I have to tell her soon. Tell her everything."

The familiar ring of his phone broke the silence. He picked it up without looking at the caller ID.

"Kyle," his mother almost purred.

Dammit. "Make it quick, Mom. I'm at work and I don't have a lot of patience today."

"Oh? At the fire station or at a modeling job?"

"I don't have time for this today, Mom. Modeling job? What are you talking about?"

The sound of papers sliding against each other came over the line. "Imagine my disappointment to get this envelope stuffed with all those unsigned contracts and a bunch of changes."

"And?"

"But at the bottom of the stack, I found these gorgeous photos."

That made him pay attention. "What photos?"

"I'm impressed. I mean, your face is partially covered, but it's obvious to me, it's you. I'd recognize that jawline anywhere. It looks just like—"

"Don't say it." He replayed stuffing those contracts in that envelope. Did he shove those pictures in too?

A long exhalation, probably from her smoking those damned cigarettes. "They're really good. What are they for? You aren't pitching yourself to another director, are you? Because if that's the case—"

"No, Mother. I'm not pitching myself to anyone."

"Pity. I could cast you in my latest project in a New York minute."

Shit. Shit. Shit. All the work he'd done to make sure she didn't find out. The less his mother knew about what was happening in Marietta, the better.

In his haste to send all the contracts back to her, he must have scooped up the proofs Charlie had given him. "It's just a fundraiser, Mom. A calendar. Nothing more."

"You'll raise plenty of funds with these photos. Goodness, *you're* a calendar. I'm so proud of you."

"No. There are a dozen guys." He paced, glancing out the front window, hoping Gabriella wouldn't arrive before he'd ended this conversation. No cars approached.

"I'm impressed that a town as small as wherever you're living right now would have enough good-looking men to fill a calendar."

He hated her elitism. "Good-looking guys live in places other than Hollywood."

"Sure, but goodness, son. Whoever took these is a wizard with the lens, not that you need much help. You're quite impressive-looking." She paused as the rustling of papers continued. "Charlotte Foster."

"How do you know the photographer's name?"

"It's on the back of the proofs. Along with her email. I must contact her about these. They are fantastic."

Shit. Shit. Fuck. "She's nice, Mom. Busy. Very busy. Probably won't get back to you anytime soon. I need to get back to work." *And off the phone before I say anything else. Stop rambling!*

"The mountain air sure does look good on you, but I need to know when you're heading south. I need you in San Antonio—"

"I'm not going."

The crunch of paper caught his attention. More than likely, she'd wadded up the contract. "Kyle, you can play pinup model anywhere. This is family."

"No, this is business. Your business." The cold wetness of the dog's nose touching his hand made him recoil.

As his mom ranted about how she had no one to depend on, Belle stared up at him with wide, hopeful eyes, making him smile.

As he scratched her behind the ears, her thick tail wagged, slamming against the side table. The impact knocked over a picture frame. Kyle reached out to right the frame, but familiar smiling faces caught his attention.

"Mom!"

"What?"

"I've already sent Dean down there. He's been checking the place out for over a week."

"I'm listening."

"If I tell you what I have planned, will you get off my back about taking over the place and read the changes I sent?"

She paused, which Kyle took as a good sign. "Okay, but I'm telling you now, there's not much you can do to change—"

"Mom. There is. And I need you to trust what I'm doing."

Chapter Nineteen

*T*ONIGHT'S THE NIGHT.

With nervous hands, Gabriella smoothed the vivid red camisole and lacy sleep shorts she'd purchased when they'd gone to Bozeman. Glancing at her watch, she knew Kyle had to be wondering what happened to her.

She'd been in here ten minutes, fretting over her breath, her bikini line, and sleep clothes, because she'd decided to take this leap of faith.

They'd already had a lovely dinner, a bottle of wine, wonderful conversation, and now it was time for dessert.

"You don't have to do this, right?" Gabriella told her reflection. Her body hummed, which pretty much answered her question. She wanted to do this. Him. Badly.

As much as her body longed for him, could her heart take it if… She shook her hands in front of her face. "Stop it. Quit overthinking. You've got a hot fireman/paramedic/military guy outside that door who wants you."

"Gabby? You okay in there?"

"I'm fine." Flashing her sexiest smile, she gave herself a

wink and opened the door to Kyle standing in the doorway of her bedroom. "You okay?"

His eyes raked over her. "I'm great. You?"

She sauntered over to the bed and crawled across it. "I'm great and—ooooff."

He caught her before she landed face first on the hardwoods. Laughing, he pulled her up on the bed and helped her sit up. "I think you overshot."

Running her fingers through her hair, she knew her face resembled the same red as her camisole. "Good grief, I was going for fantastic seduction and I ended up looking like an idiot."

"Idiots don't wear lace...whatever this is." He ran his hand along her calf then over her knee and up her thigh. "You get this yesterday?"

"Yes." His touch made her instantly forget her embarrassment. Grabbing his shirt, she pulled him toward her. "What do you think?"

"I think it's gonna be easy to take off you." He moved onto the bed, giving her a lustful stare. "But I'm gonna do it real slow."

She shivered at the idea. "Oh."

His strong hands cupped her face before he kissed her. Gently at first, pressing his lips to hers before sucking on her lower lip, coaxing her mouth open. His tongue swept in.

The rich berries of the merlot they'd finished danced across her palate as his nimble fingers moved the strap of her camisole off her shoulder.

"Kyle," she gasped as he placed kisses from her earlobe to the tender pulse points of her neck.

"Yes?"

"Did you bring, um, anything?"

He froze and sat up. "Wasn't I supposed to?"

"Yes, I simply wanted to make sure." Placing her hands on his chest, she slowly pushed him back. Her heart rate increased while she made quick work of his shirt. With a flick of her wrist, she tossed it over her shoulder.

"Animal." He sat up and helped the other strap off her shoulder, his thumbs tracing the path the straps had taken. Kissing her neck, he cupped her breast, brushing her nipple with his thumb.

She gasped as his fingers rolled danced along the sensitive flesh. "Yes."

"Take this off."

"Yes." Before she could get the camisole completely over her head, he'd taken a nipple in his mouth and suckled it. She arched into his mouth, leaving herself slightly tangled in the clothing, allowing it to serve as a temporary blindfold.

Not knowing where he'd touch her next made her body felt like it had been charged with electricity.

His tongue danced around while his fingers grazed her opposite breast. "Damn, you're beautiful."

His words floated over her skin. She allowed her top to fall away just in time to see him begin to unbutton his jeans.

Holding her hands up, she coaxed, "Let me help you with that."

He stepped off the bed and she scooted in front of him, her legs on either side of him.

Before unzipping, she ran her fingers along the outside of his pants, taunting the hard-on trapped inside.

Wetness pooled between her legs.

"Gabby," he moaned. "I've been waiting all night."

Slowly, she opened his jeans and moved them down his body. She marveled at his nakedness. The defined muscles of his arms and shoulders. The small dusting of hair on his chest, down his torso, and straight to his impressive erection. "Wow."

Reaching out, he cupped her breast, his thumb playing with her nipple before he whispered. "Turn over."

"Excuse me?"

"Don't worry. It's not that." He smiled against her skin before kissing her.

She scooted back on the bed and flipped over.

He cupped her butt and lay on top of her, kissing her back and working down her spine. The feel of his chest brushing her naked skin made her clit throb. "I need you."

"Not yet. Sit up," he cooed in her ear.

On her knees, he came up behind her and slid her shorts down. Then he took each arm as he kissed the opposite shoulder and placed her hands behind his neck. "Stay there."

His hands moved up her belly and cupped her breasts.

His thumbs made lazy, tantalizing circles across her skin.

One hand ventured south and traced the upper seam of her.

"Kyle." A moan escaped her as her hands began to fall.

He pushed them back up again. "Clasp your fingers together. Let me do the rest."

With her body aflame, she reluctantly did as he'd asked.

His erection pressed against her buttocks as his touch brought her closer to the edge.

"Kyle, that feels so good."

"I want to do one more thing. Turn around and lie down."

"You're killing me."

She repositioned, her shorts still halfway on her body.

With featherlight brushes of his lips, he kissed her, starting at the inner knee and working his way up her thigh. Somewhere in there, he stripped her of her lacy shorts before his tongue was on her clit.

Holding her hips in place, he feasted. Nibbled at the core of her sex until she thought she would cum, but he'd back away enough to keep her from falling over the edge.

Grabbing handfuls of the sheets, she writhed under him. "Please, Kyle. I need you in me."

He stood and grabbed the wrapped condom. Within seconds, he'd pulled it from the packaging, but before he could get it on, she took it and put it on him, rolling it down his shaft.

He groaned, "Gabby."

As she leaned back, he crawled onto the bed and hovered over her. Their eyes locked as he entered her in a slow, torturous move.

Gabriella thought she'd unravel right there. His presence blissfully filled her.

He growled as the tempo increased. "You feel so good, Gabby."

"Yes." She nodded as he moved in and out of her. Her all-consuming want for him drove her crazy with desire. She wrapped her legs around him, encouraging him on. "Yes."

Kyle moaned as his hips rocked quicker, harder.

She met him with each thrust, grabbing his ass, she pushing him deeper. Electricity surged through her as she came unglued. She kissed him hard and passionately rode his cock, her climax encouraging him to the finish line. "Yes, Kyle. Yes!"

He arched his back, thrusting his hips and stiffening as the pulsation of his release filled her up.

They lay in a tangled mass of arms and legs as each caught their breath.

"That was fantastic," she panted. "Truly, fan-tastic."

"Yep."

About that time, Cookie jumped on the bed and gave them a stink eye before a long meow erupted from her.

"I think that means we're supposed to move." Kyle reached over and pet the cat.

"Or she's hungry."

The tap-tap of Belle's nails on the hardwoods signaled

that more company was on the way. They laughed at the normalcy.

"I'll take care of it." Reluctantly, she unwrapped herself from his embrace, sitting on the side of the bed as she tried to locate something to cover herself.

He groaned, rolled on his back, and stretched giving her another view of his beautifully sculpted body.

Gabriella's fingers itched to roam over every chiseled line of muscle, but Belle nudged Gabriella's thigh with her cold nose. "Well, that's a buzzkill. Wet dog nose. Can I get you anything from downstairs?"

"Nope, I'm gonna clean up."

Cookie sat on something. Waving the cat away, she realized it was the shirt she'd stripped off him. Throwing it on, she ran downstairs, the animals in hot pursuit.

After a quick feeding, she stopped in the downstairs bathroom before heading back.

When she returned, she found him lying back in bed. His glorious body uncovered to the waist, but the concern on his face was a contradiction to the bliss he'd showed her not a few minutes before. "Gabby, what's this?"

She recognized it immediately. He had the letter from Riley she'd left out on her bedside table.

Dammit.

"It's nothing. I meant to put that away." She tried to grab it from him, but he held it at arm's length.

"Is this a non-disclosure agreement?"

Chapter Twenty

"Kyle, it's fine. It's done. It's not a big deal."

"A non-disclosure agreement is always a big deal. What is this about?"

She debated whether to tell him. What good would it do and would it violate the agreement of the contract?

But he wasn't associated with Winston Enterprises so what could it hurt? "My former boss stole my recipes and passed them off as his own."

He made a noise that sounded like a growl. "Gabby. What do you mean he stole from you?"

Her lips thinned. "Kyle, we just had mind-blowing sex. I don't want to talk about this right now."

"It was pretty mind-blowing, but come on. What's this about?"

Against her better judgment, she confessed, "He used my creations in several catering events and passed them off as his own. When the higher-ups would come down to give him an evaluation and he got rave reviews for the cuisine, he'd take full credit and shit on the rest of us."

The scowl on his face almost distracted her enough from

the fact the sheets had fallen off his chiseled form and lay just below his belly button.

Almost.

She licked her lips at the gorgeous creature lying there, all hers. Mentally replaying what they'd just done, her eyes raked over him and hovered around where the sheets bunched up.

"Gabby?" He wagged a finger at her. "Eyes up here."

Heat burned her skin. "Just taking in the sights."

He gave her a mischievous smirk and reached behind him, grabbing the headboard, giving her a beautiful view of his ripped body. "Take in all you want."

Her body purred. "You're not playing fair."

"What? I'm being submissive."

His lustful gaze made her squeeze her legs together. "Submissive? You're a lot of things, Kyle Cavasos, but submissive isn't one of them."

"I like to mix things up."

Walking her fingers along the edge of the bed, she slowly made her way around his side. His shirt lay loosely around her body. "You sure you want me to talk about my last job?"

"Why didn't you talk to anyone about it?" He swallowed hard as she rounded the lower corner closest to him.

Why does he want to talk about this? "Who was I going to call, Kyle? Someone I could trust and not get my family in trouble?"

"What do you mean get your family in trouble?"

Might as well tell him. "My former boss screwed me over and when he found out I tried to go above his head, he threatened to fire every single one of my family members."

"What?" That sent Kyle sitting straight up in bed. "Are you shitting me?"

"I couldn't make things complicated for them. I might have ways of making a living in other places, but my brothers, sisters, parents—they don't or can't. They want to stay in Lone Star Crossing. That's where they've been all their lives. Where my nieces and nephews go to school. Where the grandchildren live. Where they've been for generations. If they lost their jobs, their benefits, they'd lose everything. I couldn't let that happen to them."

"*You* gave everything up?"

"What was I supposed to do, Kyle?" She traced the curve of his shoulder, across his collarbone, and down his chest.

"Report it, for one. I know for a fact the owner is very pro-employee. That feels good," he moaned.

"I thought of that, but the problem with your plan is Riley is friends with Preston Crowe who hung out at the property all the time. And his dad is a famous actor."

"Jason Crowe," he snarled. "I know him. Of him."

"Whose word were they going to take? A famous friend of the manager who would bring them more business than I could make in a year or some little old Mexican cook they could replace in a heartbeat?" The words pricked her pride more than she wanted to admit. "I was nobody. I had no pull. I couldn't sue; I had no proof that he'd taken anything. He could simply tweak a spice and say it was his own creation."

"That jerk shouldn't have that kind of hold over all of you."

She drummed her fingers on her thigh before continuing. "The worst part of this is his stuck-up daughter terrorized Trinity. Made her life hell on a daily basis at school."

The muscles in his jaw clenched. "He sent his daughter after Trinity?"

As much as she appreciated his chivalry, she couldn't wrap her head around why it even mattered to him. Lone Star Crossing was thousands of miles away and, from what she could tell, he'd never set foot anywhere close. "I had no idea how evil his daughter could get, but seeing my child sobbing because of how horrible day after day had been broke my heart."

Tears welled in her eyes, but she quickly wiped them away. She'd cried enough. Now she needed to be strong for herself and her daughter. "When she came home saying she'd rather die than to go back to school, I had to protect her. She's been through enough and I'll be damned if I was going to let something like a job or him taking my recipes hurt anyone I love."

He held out his hand and pulled her toward him.

Instead of taking the seat beside him, she straddled him.

Only the bunched-up sheets between them. Squeezing her thighs together, she raised an eyebrow. "What aren't you telling me?"

"What do you mean?" He cupped her butt.

She reached around and grabbed his wrists, pinning them over his head. A useless attempt to subdue him since he could more than turn the physical tables, but he didn't struggle. In fact, the lust-filled stare he gave her told her he more than enjoyed it. "Kyle. You always sexually distract me when it's something you don't want to discuss."

"Do I?" Playfully, he tried to kiss her, but she pulled away. "Gabby. Play fair."

"Kyle. Come on. Why are you asking me about Riley? Why did you get so upset about that piece of paper?"

"I don't like seeing people I care about get screwed over." His body tensed. "Gabby, I'm sorry that happened to you, but I thought you told me Paige knew you made everything."

"She did. She and I were in the bathroom at the same time. When we were washing our hands, she noticed my uniform and commented on the food. I told her they were my recipes and she complimented me on them. Joked about me buying the diner."

"When did you find out about Riley stealing your ideas?"

"There was another employee in the bathroom. She told him what I'd said; he confronted me. I bit back; he fired me—told me if I said anything to anyone about it, he would make sure no person in my family would be able to find a job in a one-hundred-mile radius." Frustration took over and she began to move off him, but his hands held her in place.

"Stay. Talk to me." The calm in his voice was an eerie contradiction to the fury in his eyes.

"What's the point? It's done and I'm here."

The sexy all but disappeared from his eyes as a quick wave of anger crossed his face. "Did he…hurt you?"

Releasing him from her grasp, she sat back. "Are you asking if he tried to assault me?"

"Yes."

"He made multiple passes at me and some crude comments, but he never forced himself."

His body tensed underneath her. "I see. Did he do this often?"

Gabriella rolled her eyes. "He did it enough to be inappropriate."

"I'll kill him."

"Get a grip, Kyle. Why would you even bother?"

"Because I love you, that's why."

Chapter Twenty-One

H E HONESTLY HADN'T meant to say it.
Ever.

To anyone.

But those three words slipped right out without a thought in his head.

Her eyebrows hit her hairline. "What did you say?"

Flipping her on her back, he hovered over her, taking in every feature of her face.

The way her mouth curled up when she laughed.

The mocha brown of her eyes.

The smoothness of her skin.

She'd bewitched him—body, heart, and soul.

Her eyes were wide with worry. "Kyle?"

"I love you." *Dammit, what are you doing? You said it again.*

"What?"

Brushing his lips against hers, he whispered, "I love you, Gabriella Marcos."

"You…you love…*me?*"

Now, after the third time, the words didn't feel like glass

sliding along his throat. They felt natural.

Real.

Perfect.

Of course, his guts twisted tight since she hadn't said anything in return. *Time to up the stakes.* "*Te amo.*"

A nervous smile spread across her face as she placed her hands on his cheeks. "Kyle. You learned some Spanish for me?"

"I know some. My grandmother and dad spoke Spanish."

"You cheater!" She squirmed playfully underneath him as she rattled off Spanish phrases he could only understand parts of.

"I love you." His words breathless kisses along the tender valley between her ear and collarbone.

A moan escaped her as she ran her hands up his arms and dug her fingers into his back. "Show me how much you love me."

With one swift move, he was inside her again.

Despite his desire to feel the bliss of release, he took his time, bringing her to orgasm before his own.

As they basked in the afterglow, she rested her head on his chest, and whispered, "I love you, Kyle Cavasos."

His heart fluttered with angst. *You have to tell her. You have to tell her everything.*

His fingers caressed her hair as his mind raced with fury about what that piece of shit Riley had put her through.

She gave up everything to save her family.

His heart ached for what she'd sacrificed. Even though the situation brought her to Marietta, to him and this moment, he wanted to make things right.

Even if it meant she might leave.

Chapter Twenty-Two

WITH JONAH FINALLY posing for the calendar, Charlie had set up the wrap-up party at Grey's later that afternoon.

Gabriella, like a lot of other women in this town, couldn't wait to see the photos.

Seeing all those guys in one room would certainly boost sales and finish the fundraising for Harry's House.

Charlie had already mentioned the social media traffic was keeping her more than busy.

Gabriella checked in on the website and social media accounts several times. She noticed that Kyle had the least amount of coverage. When Charlie came into the diner to get a takeout order, Gabriella asked her about it. She explained Kyle had asked his presence be minimal and if it had been up to him, he would have asked to not be on any public forums, but having a calendar with only eleven guys made no sense.

According to Charlie, social media was already buzzing about the project and there had been several marriage proposals on his pictures, some with hashtag #JasonCroweLookalike in the comments.

Cringing, Gabriella commented that there were far better people to compare her lover to than that full-time adulterer.

But no matter. As far as she was concerned, even having one of those handsome men selling a calendar of himself would be sufficient to raise plenty of money.

Like her favorite new month, October.

And Mr. October sat right in front of her, having his morning coffee and reading while she finished up the morning rush.

"What?" he asked before taking a drink of his coffee.

"Nothing." She rested her elbows on the counter as she stared at him. Gently taking the mug from his hands, she took a sip. "Just taking in the view."

Kyle gave her a sexy wink. "Take it in all you want. It's all yours."

Mine. Those words couldn't have sounded sweeter if she wanted them to. Somehow, someway, she'd managed to gain the attention of the hottest guy in town.

How ironic that things are so amazing when our first introduction was me sitting on the pooper.

The sun spilled into the room through the window blinds, highlighting some of the crumbs on the ground and tables that had been left by the morning rush.

Annie Scott swept under one of the tables as Casey checked the napkin dispensers. Flo would be in later today to cover for Gabriella when she went to the wrap-up party.

Merlin sang an old George Strait song as he worked in the kitchen.

Other than the staff, Kyle, and Gabriella, the only other people in the place were Keely and Lucy, who sat in a corner booth, talking. Keely had finished a huge plate of pancakes, eggs, and bacon while Lucy ordered a small breakfast and drank coffee faster than a fish drank water.

The smell of chocolate drifted out from the kitchen. Gabriella checked the time and handed his coffee back. "Oh, the brownies are done."

"Don't run out of those. There'll be a riot if you do."

Pride tickled her throat as she removed the pans from the oven and placed them on the counter. Her Spicy Brownies were an overnight hit. Every day, she'd sell out. Dozens of them.

Along with the orange-glazed cinnamon bread she'd added to the breakfast menu and now sold by the loaves, Gabriella's first couple of weeks' profits had slightly exceeded her expectations.

Pulling out the ancho sprinkles and the powdered sugar mix, she began setting up for plating and topping the desserts.

Annie and Casey waved her away from the brownie prep.

"Go, get back out there to your hunka-hunka-burnin' love." Casey pointed. "We've got this."

Annie gave a thumbs-up.

Giddy with excitement, she returned to the counter. Kyle

continued to read a *National Geographic* magazine as she replaced half-full salt and pepper shakers with full ones before rolling more silverware.

She marveled at the broadness of his shoulders. How his hair looked the same color as sand when the sun hit it just right.

The green of his eyes. How lust-filled they became when he made love to her.

In fact, she'd like nothing more than to crawl on top of his body right now and give him an early afternoon delight.

"What time is the event at Grey's?" Her finger traced along his wrist.

His eyebrow cocked up. "Why?"

"Because—"

A low vibrating hum sounded. He pulled out his phone and glanced at the screen before sliding his thumb across it. "Let me check on something. Need to go outside. Be right back."

She watched him and his perfect backside move across the room. As he walked away from her, that familiar, delicious tingle danced across her body and settled between her thighs.

Mine! All mine. Never in a million years would she have guessed she'd be heart-deep in love with a man from Montana, but here they were.

In love.

She was the boss of her own diner.

Her daughter had found her niche.

Life couldn't have been any sweeter.

Before he exited, Kyle walked over to Keely and Lucy.

Keely had sustained a head injury last week and he'd been one of the guys who'd gotten her to the hospital in one piece.

She gave him a stiff smile as her hands protectively rested across her belly. After the amount of food she'd taken in today, Keely should be more than stuffed.

It's like she's eating for two. Uh-oh.

Lucy sat up straight as though she were about to say something as Kyle talked to them.

A fierceness boiled in Gabriella's gut at how the women looked at him, but her rational brain calmed her angst.

Remember, he hadn't dated anyone else in town before you came along. Cheating isn't in his nature.

Without warning, Deputy Logan popped his head in the door. A look of relief on his face when he saw Kyle.

They needed him for a search and rescue up on the mountain and he had only a few minutes to make it to the helipad at the hospital.

Watching Kyle's face light up when Logan gave him a quick rundown, Gabriella smiled. He obviously loved doing his job. Helping people. Making this a better world.

If that alone isn't sexy, I don't know what is.

With a quick wave, Kyle headed out, but promised to be at Grey's that afternoon.

Such is the life of the girlfriend of an adrenaline junkie.

With hardly anyone there, Lucy's voice carried easily. When she asked Keely if Kyle reminded her of anyone, her friend shook her head.

For the next several minutes Gabriella, Casey, and Annie cleaned up and restocked the restaurant as they got it ready for lunch.

Merlin quickly set up the kitchen, trading out breakfast foods for the midday and early dinner crowds.

Keely and Lucy went on their way as the first new customers wandered in.

The next couple of hours went by in a blur.

They sold out of the first batch of Spicy Brownies by eleven-thirty just as the next batch came out of the oven.

By the time Gabriella had a chance to look at the clock again, it was two thirty. She sat in her office, entered the day's sales into the spreadsheet, and checked inventory before Flo arrived at four.

Quickly, Gabriella went home, cleaned up, and picked up Trinity before heading to Grey's.

"Mom, can I just go do my homework at the diner instead of going to Grey's?" Trinity asked.

Out of the corner of her eye, Gabriella noticed Tia and Frederick walking up the sidewalk along with another boy.

"Got a study date?"

Twirling her hair between her long fingers, Trinity nodded. "Yes, we have a big project due in science and—"

Waving her off, Gabriella laughed, "Go. Be smart. Be

amazing."

"Thanks, Mom." The teen took off and met her friends in front of the diner. They all smiled and talked for a moment before the newcomer opened the door for all of them to go inside.

Hope wrapped around Gabriella's heart just as a very long limo cruised by and turned right at Court Street.

"Pretentious. Probably going to the Graff." The steady beat of music spilled out into the street as soon as she opened the door to Grey's. Within seconds of her walking in, she locked eyes with Kyle. He wasted no time greeting her with a quick kiss.

"Wow, this is quite a turnout." Gabriella pointed. A country band played as people moved about the room. Balloons were tied on the backs of chairs and wait staff moved about, trying to keep up with drink orders.

Large prints of the chosen pictures for the calendar were on display on the far wall. She stopped in front of Kyle's and marveled at the chiseled features of his body.

"Michelangelo couldn't have done a better job if he'd sculpted you out of marble," she mumbled.

His hand rested on the small of her back then slid down and cupped her butt. "Flatterer. You just want to get lucky, again."

"You know I do."

ER doctor Gavin Clark joined them as he slapped Kyle on the back. "You should hear about what this guy did today."

Gabriella interlaced her fingers with Kyle's. "What did he do?"

"Went out and helped bring in a girl who'd been living up on the mountain for a good two months."

She felt her eyebrows lift to her hairline. "You did? She okay?"

"She's fine. Smart kid." Kyle pulled out his phone and scowled. His thumb sailed across the screen and he tucked it back into his pocket. "Gavin got her stabilized when we got her to the hospital."

"Yeah, but you did the heavy lifting. Great job." He patted Kyle on the back before joining a couple of other first responders across the room.

Kyle kept looking at his phone and then at the door. His jaw clenched. "Shit."

She threaded her arm through his. "Kyle, are you okay?"

"Fine." The door opened and he scowled, but after Jonah walked in, Kyle relaxed. "Let's get out of here. I need to talk to you."

Her body hummed. "Talk, huh? Is that what we're calling it now?"

The corner of his mouth twitched. "No, Gabby. I really need to talk to you."

"Right now? But the party—" He pulled her outside, leaving the loud music and conversations behind.

"Kyle, are you okay?"

His forehead furrowed as he looked around. "Anyone at the diner right now?"

"Not many people. It's right before the dinner run."

Without letting go of her hand, he walked quickly toward her work. "Can we talk in your office?"

Worry lodged in her chest. "Kyle, what's going on?"

"I'll tell you in a minute. Need to get somewhere he won't see us."

"Who?"

They entered the diner and made a beeline for her office. As soon as the door closed behind them, she grabbed him by the shoulders. "What is going on?"

His fists clenched at his sides. "Gabby. There's something I need to tell you about me."

"Okay. What is it?"

A knock at the door interrupted them. Before she could open it, Trinity poked her head in. "Mom?"

"Yes, sweetie."

"You need to come out here."

"Can it wait?"

Trinity's eyes darted from her mother to Kyle. "Not really."

"Fine."

As she followed her daughter out into the main area, Kyle grabbed her arm. "Gabby, before you go out there, I need you to listen to me."

"Honey, it's going to be fine. Let me take care of whatever this is, first. Then you'll have my full, undivided attention."

As she walked through the swinging doors, she noticed everyone in the room looked like they'd been electrocuted. All standing wide-eyed, slack-jawed, and staring at a man in the doorway.

"Guys, what is going on?" Gabriella felt Kyle's hand on her shoulder. "T, what did I need to see?"

"More like who." She not so subtly pointed.

A broad-shouldered man in the doorway smirked. His smooth-as-honey voice filled the room. "Kyle, you're a hard man to find. Glad I caught you before you moved."

"Moved? Kyle what is he…talking about?" Standing in the doorway was the last person Gabriella ever thought she'd see in her diner.

Jason Crowe.

The man held out his arms and smiled. "Hello, son."

Son? Did Jason Crowe just call my boyfriend son?

Chapter Twenty-Three

"DID JASON CROWE just call Kyle *son*?" Flo leaned over and failed in her attempt to be quiet.

The scene reminded Gabriella of those screwball comedies of the Golden Age of Hollywood, but when she faced Kyle, the scowl told her everything she needed to know.

"He's your father?"

With his fists at his sides, Kyle moved toward him. "What are you doing, here, *Jason*?"

"I thought Patrick was your father."

"It's a complicated story, sweetheart." Casually removing his sunglasses and tucking them into the front coat pocket of his perfectly tailored suit, Jason smirked. "Your mother told me you had some photo shoot party for your charity work. I decided to come in. Support the cause."

A growl escaped Kyle as he mocked, "Support the cause. You're full of shit."

Flo gasped. "I can't believe he'd talk to that handsome hunk of man that way."

Biting her lip, Gabriella stopped the shocked laughter that threatened to break the palatable tension. *Who would have thought Flo had a thing for movie stars?*

With a casual shrug, Jason stood like he had during many red-carpet events. "Maybe, but me mentioning it on my social media pages an hour ago has certainly gotten a lot of buzz. I bet you raise enough by Monday to help pay for everything that place needs and more."

"I didn't need your help with this," Kyle's snapped. "I didn't ask for your help."

"I know, but PR is PR, son. You should know that by now." Sauntering forward, Jason Crowe held all the confidence of many of the characters he'd played on-screen. He ran his fingers along one of the tables and cringed when he held his hand up.

His confidence reeked more of arrogance than self-assurance.

Seeing him in person, Gabriella couldn't be less impressed. Still, Kyle's father?

Glancing over his shoulder at her, she watched anger burn in Kyle's eyes.

He quickly looked away. "You mean you wanted to get your picture taken for something that made you look human after cheating on your wife."

Seeing the two side by side, the resemblance couldn't be more obvious.

Same color eyes.

Same broad-shouldered stature.

Same chiseled jawline.

I feel like a moron. Gabriella moved behind the counter.

Trinity and her friends slowly sat back down at their corner table as Annie, Merlin, and Casey all stood, looking out the kitchen pass-through window. Everyone had bright looks of anticipation on their faces, like they were watching that climactic moment of a movie.

Maybe I should make popcorn.

Drumming his fingers on the back of a chair, Jason continued, "I've already had three of my entertainment writer friends contact me about it. They want to do a write-up. You know. Hit it like a father and son—"

"I am not your son!" Kyle screamed. "Patrick was my father. Always has been. Always will be."

The charm from Jason's face wavered. "How many times are we going to have this conversation? Huh? Whether you like it or not, I am your dad."

Shaking his head, Kyle said nothing.

A bit of confidence faded with Kyle's reaction. "Look. I'm sorry. Patrick was a good man and he deserved to find out sooner than he did, but it is what it is."

Kyle remained stoically silent.

"Aren't you going to say anything?" Shifting his weight, Jason flashed a movie-star smile. "Kyle. Son."

Holding his hands up, Kyle moved away. "You've made an appearance. You've posted on social media. Again, you've screwed up my life. Time for you to go."

"It's been years since I've talked to you. What—you

don't have time to sit and talk with your old—"

"Don't."

He lied to me. The words rolled over and over in her mind like the surf slapping the beach.

He's Jason Crowe's son. He lied.

Blinking back tears, she reined in her anger. She wouldn't give Kyle the satisfaction of seeing her meltdown.

"And who is this?" Jason's smooth words pulled her out of her pity party.

He flashed his overly white smile and gave her a wink. "I don't believe I've met you yet."

Moving in front of Gabriella, Kyle blocked his father's view. "Get lost, Jason. She's not your type."

"Oh, and what is my type, *son*?"

"Married and desperate."

"That's not fair, Kyle. There's a lot more to that story than you know."

"I doubt it."

She peeked around Kyle's shoulders, the very shoulders she'd clutched as they made love last night. *Dammit, even when I'm furious at him, I can't get my mind out of the gutter.*

As soon as he made eye contact with her, a slow smirk spread across Jason's over-tanned face. "Well, for her, I could make an exception."

"You're a disgusting human being," Gabriella snapped.

"Gabriella! Now that's no way to treat our guest." Flo patted the back of her hair and quickly checked her breath.

Jason's charms obviously worked on her, but Gabriella had seen plenty of guys like this before. He was no different than Derrick.

Riley.

All self-important jerks who think the world owes them for simply existing. "You need to leave."

Jason looked like he'd been Tasered. "Did you tell me to leave?"

Kyle locked his arms across his chest. "She said you're disgusting, Jason."

Lifting a shoulder, Jason strolled forward. "Maybe, but no one's perfect."

Without pause, Gabriella rebutted, "Oh, you're far from perfect, Mr. Crowe."

"Call me Jason."

"Okay, I'll call you Jason," Flo shot out from behind the counter and escorted him to a table. "What would you like to drink, Jason? We have several specials, Jason."

Trinity's study group began to giggle and Tia started taking pictures with her phone.

"Good Lord." Kyle patted Flo on the shoulder. "Flo, he's not that big of a deal."

Flashing Flo a red-carpet smile, Jason held his hand out to her. "Jason Crowe."

"I know." She giggled like a schoolgirl being asked to the prom.

If the situation weren't so ridiculous, Gabriella might

find some humor in it, but the only thing she could focus on was Kyle's deception.

Like father. Like son.

"Gabby doesn't like you," Kyle growled.

"But everybody likes me."

Gabriella scoffed, "No one likes a man who blatantly cheats on his family and brags about it."

That stopped Jason in his tracks. "No one talks to me like that. No one."

"If you're going to be in my diner, get used to it."

"I see."

A shiver went up her spine at how eerily similar father and son sounded when they said those two words. *How else were they alike?*

He took a step forward, but out of the corner of her eye, she watched Kyle lean toward Jason.

That stopped the movie star in his tracks. For a moment, no one moved, but when he clasped his hands in front of him, he gave Flo a smile. "So, Flo, what's good here?"

Before Flo could rattle off the specials, Kyle grabbed his father by the arm and dragged him out of the diner. "Nope, you need to go."

As the door closed, a giggle caught Gabriella's attention.

Flo looked like a schoolgirl. "Oh my. He's even better-looking in person."

"I guess. I can't get past the fact he keeps cheating on his family." *Or the fact he's Kyle's father.*

"I didn't say I wanted to date the man, Gabriella. He's a scoundrel for certain, but nothin' says I can't look at the merchandise."

Despite her general confusion and frustration, Gabriella couldn't help but laugh at Flo's honesty.

Glancing out the window, she watched Kyle and Jason argue on the sidewalk. Her heart sunk at her lover's deception.

He didn't trust me enough to tell me who he was. What else hasn't he told me?

She dried her face with the back of her hand and turned away from the window.

"I'll be in the office." She'd barely shut the door before tears fell so fast, she couldn't see.

Chapter Twenty-Four

"GET THE HELL out of here. Out of my life." Kyle screamed loud enough for people across the street to look in the direction of the commotion.

"You need to calm down."

"I've got a chance to have a good life and I don't need you showing up or Mom giving me some guilt trip to take over any of her properties."

"A life? Here? With that girl in there?"

"She's one of the best people I know. Dammit, why are you such a snob?" Running his fingers through his hair, Kyle had to silently tell himself not to rip it all out. "At least I know she won't dump me as soon as she sees you, so put your dick away."

"What is that supposed to mean?" Jason locked his arms over his chest as a thin line of perspiration beaded on his upper lip.

"You know damned well what it means."

"You think I stole your girlfriends?"

"No, you didn't have to steal anything. If you walked into a room, they were more than willing to stray your way."

The many hits Kyle's pride took every time a woman he liked turned her focus to his famous father weighed on his heart.

"If it makes you feel any better, I didn't screw any of them."

Jason's words hit him harder than seeing the man here in the first place.

"What do you mean, you never slept with—"

"What? You think I'd sink so low as to fuck my son's girlfriends?" Glaring at Kyle, Jason pointed his finger at him. "As soon as I'd see those sluts jump off you and head to me, I'd show them the door. Every time. No one does that to my son."

Confusion rolled around with everything he thought he knew about his…Jason.

Shaking his head, Jason smirked. "I know you don't think much of me and that's fine. I didn't think much of my father, either."

"You are not my father."

Frustration replaced amusement. "Like it or not, I am, but Patrick was your dad."

"Until he found out he wasn't." That had never been anything he planned to admit to anyone.

"What are you talking about? Patrick was a good man."

"He was and he was a wounded one. Things were never the same after…after…the cancer."

The self-assurance of the movie star faded as the concern

of a father replaced it. "Your mother never said anything. Was he abusive?"

"No, he wasn't cruel. Just disappointed. In me."

"I see."

Again, Kyle wondered why a charity calendar shoot with his bastard child would bring Jason to Marietta. "Why are you here?"

"To make amends."

A dark idea nestled in Kyle's brain. "Are you dying?"

"No. No, nothing like that. Quite simply, the other son I have is a complete fuckup."

"Preston? Hell, I could have told you that years ago." Kyle stuffed his hands in his jeans pockets. "And what?"

"You've done amazing things and you keep doing them. That's not me. That's Patrick."

The kind words only antagonized Kyle's wounded pride. "Great. You've said your piece. Now what are you going to come up with to apologize to me because I couldn't save him? Because I wasn't a match?" The confession surprised even Kyle. He turned his back and tried to get control over his long-ignored anger.

"Damn, son. I'm sorry."

As he shook his head, Kyle's frustration festered. "That doesn't change anything, does it?"

"Even if Patrick fathered you, there's no guarantee that you would have matched."

Spinning on his heels, he growled, "Guess we'll never

know, will we? Because he's dead."

Jason's face flushed an angry red. "You know what? I've had enough of this. I get that you're pissed at me. I betrayed my best friends. Your mother and father, but I'm not going to apologize for being half of you."

"And why's that, Jason?"

"Because you're a damned fine human being."

"You're going to take credit for me?"

"No, I only gave the genes. I know who you are is because of Patrick." Leaning against the light pole, Jason's confidence waned. "He was my best friend. A good man. Great man, and I let my dick get in the way of our friendship. Of the friendship I had with your mother. He didn't deserve the fallout from that. None of you did."

This had been the longest conversation Kyle had ever had with Jason Crowe. "No, we didn't."

He pointed toward the diner. "That woman in there. She loves you. You."

"After this, I'm pretty sure I've fucked this up."

"What do you mean?"

"I lied to her."

"About what?"

"Me." Quickly, Kyle gave his father the five-minute version of meeting Gabriella, her family, the resort, Riley, and how far he'd fallen in love with her and what he'd planned to do to make sure he could stay in Marietta. Not that it mattered now. "She's not going to talk to me after this."

"You kidding me? Did you see how pissed she was when I mocked you? If she could have, she would have ripped my eyes out." A sly smirk spread across his father's face. "Seeing her unimpressed with me should be a good sign. She loves you. And you'd better fight like hell to keep her."

"Why should I listen to what you have to say about marriage?"

"Because I didn't fight for my family and I regret it every day of my life." Squeezing Kyle's shoulder, Jason coaxed, "Go on, son. Get in there. Make it right."

For once, the men agreed on something.

"I plan to." Extending his hand, Kyle soaked in the first true talk he'd ever had with Jason. "Thanks. I'm still pissed at you."

"Fair enough." Responding in kind, Jason shook Kyle's hand before heading toward the Graff Hotel.

Chapter Twenty-Five

"YOU LIED TO me!" Gabriella snapped as she stormed around her small office. "Why couldn't you have told me who you were? And you're moving?"

"I'm sorry. You know how hard all of this is for me?"

"What's hard, Kyle? Being the son of a famous movie star? Sounds like a terribly hard life. The idea of little ole me thinking this…this was anything real. Important."

He hated that he'd hurt her. Lied. "I think you're real important."

"Oh, please. You have your pick of Hollywood hotties and you want to stay with little ole me?"

"Do you know how many women have tried to get to my parents through me? Do you have any idea what it's like never knowing if anyone wants you for what you've accomplished or if they are just trying to get a glimpse into this fake world that everyone seems to think is so great?"

"No, I don't. But you could have told me something at some point. I gave you plenty of chances to say something and every time you'd find some delicious distraction." She sighed as her eyes betrayed her and scanned him. "No, no, we're going to talk about this."

Biting his lip, he laughed at her obvious libido. "You're right. I know you're mad."

She shook her head. "I'm beyond mad. I'm livid."

"What was I supposed to do, Gabby? If I'd told you I was Jason Crowe's son, what would you have done?"

"I would have dumped you. Right then. Right there. No questions asked."

That answer surprised him. "Why?"

"Because a man like that, like him, like Derrick—they don't know what relationships are about. They are simply notches on a bedpost for them. Nothing more."

The corner of his mouth twitched at her honesty. How he loved the way she stood her ground. Loved how she wasn't impressed with his genetics. Loved…her.

He'd said it, but for the first time in his adult life, loving someone didn't scare the hell out of him. In fact, loving her felt like the only rational thing in his world. "Dump me because Jason Crowe's my dad. You'd be the first."

"This isn't funny, Kyle. I trusted you."

"Do you blame me for saying nothing? Do you know how many women have tried to get to know me because of my family? Hoping my mother would cast them in a movie."

"Your mother? Who the hell is your mother?"

"Lillian Winston."

"Holy shit!" Her hand slapped over her mouth. "The Lillian Winston? Like Winston Resorts and Spas?"

"Yes."

"The director and producer?"

"That's her."

"As if you couldn't be more pedigreed." She stormed out of the office, but stopped short of the swinging doors. "Is that why you've been asking me about the resort?"

He shoved his hands in his pockets. "I'm supposed to take over the place by October."

"What happens if you don't?"

"I lose my share of my grandfather's inheritance, but—"

"That's great. You're leaving. I've got to get to work." She turned her back on him and ventured into the busy dining room.

The waitresses ran in and out of the back, grabbing orders. After the Jason Crowe sighting, it was standing-room only as people waited for tables. They had to call in Griffin to help his brother, Merlin, with the orders.

Trinity and her friends bussed tables and washed dishes to keep up with the traffic.

Gabby walked from table to table, filling waters, clearing plates, and facing away from Kyle.

He didn't relent, but followed her as she walked to the back and put the dishes in the sink. "Gabby, talk to me."

"What are you doing in Marietta? With me?"

"I told you. My dad brought me here—"

"So that wasn't a lie?"

"No, everything I have told you is true." His heart

thumbed hard against his ribs.

Her eyes glistened with unshed tears. "But you didn't tell me everything, did you?"

"No."

"Is there anything else?"

"Not that I can think of." He grabbed her hand and held it to his chest. "Dammit, Gabby, I love you. I want to be there to protect you and Trinity. Why won't you let me do that?"

"Because lying is a deal breaker for me, Kyle."

"I'm sorry. I couldn't tell you anything—"

She pulled away. "I get it. You were protecting yourself too, but I can't be with someone who's willing to lie about who he is. Who doesn't trust me enough to tell me his real name."

"Is this because of Jason? I'm not Jason."

"I know you're not Jason, but…but…I need to work. Please, go."

When she walked in the back, his heart fell to his feet.

"Give her time, honey. She's mad as a hornet right now, but let her cool off." Flo patted his back. "For now, make yourself scarce and clear your head."

Reluctantly, he walked out, his heart all but broken.

Chapter Twenty-Six

THE EVENING RUSH had been its busiest ever. By the end of the night, all the waitresses happily counted their tips and left thrilled with the traffic.

Griffin and Merlin cleaned up the back and headed out.

Trinity's study group had left a couple of hours ago and she'd moved to the far end of the counter. As she finished her homework, she sipped her herbal tea.

"Ready to go home, sweetie?" Gabriella began turning off lights when the front door opened.

"Sorry, we're closed."

"Mom," Trinity snapped.

"Yes, I know, but I was hoping to talk to you for a moment." The woman's smooth-as-silk voice drifted over the room.

"Mom, you should really—"

"Trinity, please." Annoyance seeped into every pore. The last thing Gabriella wanted was to talk to anyone else. Attempting to massage the knots out of her neck, Gabriella mentally counted to ten before dealing with some stranger who wouldn't get the message.

"Mom." Trinity snapped her fingers, again. "Seriously."

"Ma'am, I'm sorry, but—" Turning, Gabriella couldn't believe who stood in front of her.

Lillian Winston. And she looked more beautiful than her photo that hung in the main administrative offices of the resort.

A slow, smirk spread across her face. Her beautiful green eyes focused in on Gabriella. "I'd truly appreciate a moment of your time, Ms. Marcos."

This day couldn't get any more surreal.

"Well, I stand corrected." Motioning her over to the counter, Trinity moved her books over as Kyle's mother gracefully sat down.

"Thank you."

"What can I get you this evening, Ms. Winston?"

"It's Mrs. Cavasos. I go by my maiden name professionally." Laying her Hermès bag on the chair next to her, she asked, "May I have a cup of coffee and some of those brownies my son's been bragging about."

His name hit Gabriella straight in the heart. "He's been bragging about my desserts?"

She chuckled. "He's been bragging about a lot of things, especially you."

Trinity joined in on the amusement. "Well, he's been over enough."

"And you must be Trinity. Kyle tells me you're quite the artist."

The teen's eyebrows hit her hairline. "Oh, I guess he's…I…I do pretty well."

"Better than well from what I hear. Kyle says you're a star on the rise." Reaching across Trinity, Lillian tapped the sketchbook. "May I see your work?"

With nervous hands, Trinity opened the pages and explained each of her latest drawings while Gabriella started another pot of coffee.

Over the next several minutes, Gabriella watched her daughter's increasing excitement as she explained her sketches while Lillian asked thoughtful questions of each piece.

Despite the kindness of her words, that gave little comfort to Gabriella when talking to the famous Lillian Winston. She'd read enough of the company's memos, magazine articles, and newsletters to know how much of a force of nature the strong-willed Ms. Winston could be. Even from here, Gabriella saying the wrong thing could hurt her family. "What can I do for you, Ms. Winston, I mean, Mrs. Cavasos?"

Pulling a large envelope out of her bag, she placed it in front of her as she clasped her hands and rested them on top. "Ms. Marcos, I've read your file."

"You have?" Gabriella felt like she was trying to swallow a boulder. *Lord knows what Riley put in there.* "And?"

"I want to thank you."

"Excuse me?" She opened the envelope. Among the papers was a check. "What's this?"

"A bonus. Because of you and your family, my grandfather's first hotel hasn't tanked."

Holy cow. This is a year's salary. "You're...welcome?"

"Mr. Fitzgerald had quite a good time trying to ruin my favorite property, but he's been sent on his way and neither you nor your family will never hear from him again."

"I didn't see that coming." Her hands trembled as she tried to pour herself some coffee. "I understand Kyle is supposed to take over the place."

"He was, but he's changed his mind."

"What do you mean?"

"He's asked that your siblings help run the place instead."

The coffee mug slipped from her hands and clanked on the saucer. "What?"

"He promoted your brother, Joaquin, to director of the grounds and Edwardo to director of maintenance. Your mother will run the entire salon and spa."

"*And* the spa?" She could only imagine her mother's face when she received the news. *Her screams of excitement should have been heard all the way here.*

"Yes and Kyle insisted we review their files as well as all the employees' files of the resort since Riley arrived. No one had received a raise or bonus since he'd been there." She sipped her coffee, leaving a perfect imprint of pink lips on the rim of the cup. "In fact, he'd been pocketing more than his fair share of bonuses and from what I understand, he'd been quite the little tyrant. Not to mention, Preston, Jason's useless excuse for a son has been using my resort as his own bachelor pad. Jason's not going to like getting that bill."

"I'm glad to have that taken care of." Tears of relief ran down her face. "I was so worried about them. Now I won't have to."

"Every member of your family who has worked at that resort has been loyal and hardworking. They've more than earned that." She took another elegant sip. "And now they are part owners."

"What did you say?"

Clasping her hands in her lap, Lillian calmly replied, "Kyle insisted that they were given not only promotions, but stock options and part ownership."

"Oh, my gosh!" Trinity clapped her hands in front of her face. "That's incredible."

"Why?" Gabriella's heart beat so fast, she had to catch her breath. "Not that I'm not grateful, but why would he do that?"

The corner of Lillian's perfect mouth twitched. "Isn't it obvious? My son loves you. Wants you and your family happy. Safe."

"But I thought he had to run it to keep his inheritance." Without warning, Gabriella's bottom lip quivered at the joy that surrounded her like a blanket. "I can't believe he did that."

"He figured out a way around the restriction in the will.

All it said was he had to effectively run the resort. That can also include him hiring reliable people to do it instead seeing over the day-to-day operations." A sly smile spread across Lillian's face as she continued. "My son has always found a smart way to get what he wants. He's smart to a fault."

The idea of her family owning a piece of the business they'd poured their hearts and souls into overwhelmed Gabriella, making it hard for her to breathe. She patted her chest to calm her rising heart rate. "I can't believe this. They will be okay."

Trinity nodded as her eyes sparkled and she grabbed her phone. "That means Sheila is gone too."

Sliding the half empty coffee mug over, Lilliana continued. "Please don't think I've forgotten what happened to you, Ms. Marcos."

"What do you mean?"

"Before I even talked to Kyle, Paige Sheenan of Tutro Enterprises called me herself to say how amazing the food was at that retreat they had last month."

"She's a lovely woman." Grabbing a napkin, Gabriella dried her eyes.

"I know Riley stole from you, threatened to fire you and your family if you didn't quit. His daughter made your Trinity's life hell and he wouldn't work with you to better the situation."

A clunk of something on the counter made them both turn.

Trinity gasped her hands still open from where she held her phone. "Mom, he did that to you? You didn't tell me any of this."

Turning in her body slightly, the elegant woman continued. "Your mother even went so far to sign a non-disclosure and non-competition agreement so she could never advertise the recipes you used."

"Mom? Why would you do that?"

How she'd hoped she'd never have to explain it. With the owner sitting here and being more than approachable, Gabriella realized she could have pushed harder to make things right. But there's no guarantee they would have the same results. "I had to protect you, Trinity. All of you."

"*Abuela*, Uncle Edwardo, Uncle Joaquin? Did they know?"

"None of them knew because they'd all quit. Give up everything they'd earned. I couldn't do that to them."

Her daughter ran around the counter and pulled her into her arms. "I'm sorry I didn't make things easy for you when we first got here."

"Thank you, T. It was hard for both of us." Gabriella soaked in her daughter's hug. It had been a long time since Trinity hugged her like this and it was painfully obvious the girl had passed her in height. "Ugh, I can't believe you're taller than I am."

"Can I get one of those amazing Spicy Brownies I've been hearing about?" Lillian asked as soon as the women stepped apart.

"Of course. Allow me." Trinity nodded and darted into the back.

As soon as the swinging doors closed, Lillian reached out and patted Gabriella's hand. "My son. He cares very much for you. Dare I say, he's completely in love with you."

A heaviness sat in Gabriella's heart. "Yes, that's what he said."

"And you don't believe him?"

"Ms. Winston—"

She wagged a finger. "It's Mrs. Cavasos. Mrs. Patrick Cavasos."

The pain in the woman's eyes didn't go unnoticed. It was the same pain Gabriella had seen in Kyle's eyes when he spoke of his father. "Mrs. Cavasos. I mean no disrespect, but this conversation is really between Kyle and myself."

With a very familiar smirk, Lillian raised a perfectly groomed eyebrow. "Touché, Gabriella, but I do want you to understand something."

"Yes, ma'am?"

"My son is a passionate individual. He always has been. When he wants something, he works very hard for it and when he invests his heart, he doesn't hold back."

Trinity returned with three plates and sat down after placing them each accordingly. "One for each of us."

"Thank you, dear." Lillian stirred her coffee in lazy circles. "I pushed hard for him to leave Marietta and take over that Winston property. I almost had him convinced to leave, but then he met you."

"Me?" With trembling hands, she tried to drink her coffee but ended up splattering it on the brownie. "Good grief."

A giggle from her daughter as Trinity handed Gabriella a napkin.

"It was like trying to push a bolder uphill. He found a way to keep the resort running profitably, fulfill his grandfather's request, *and* stay here, with you."

Her heart melted, but his lies still hurt. "As much as I appreciate knowing this, I do worry that he's like—"

"His father?"

"I mean no disrespect."

"He's exactly like his father."

Lillian might as well have punched Gabriella in the gut. "And that's a good thing? I'm a bit confused."

Wiping away a tear, she sniffed. "Patrick Cavasos was as good of a man as anyone could be. Other than my son, there's no man who would even come close to measuring up."

As endearing and honest as Lillian's words were, Gabriella worried. "But I thought Mr. Crowe was…"

Shaking her head, Lillian picked up a brownie and nibbled the edge. "Jason and I made a mistake. It was a hard time for Patrick and I. We fought a lot. Money was tough. We had one child and I'd miscarried."

"I'm so sorry. Kyle never told me that part."

"I never told him. I'm sure I had postpartum depression,

but no one talked about it back then and Patrick didn't know what to do." She casually lifted a shoulder. "I needed someone to talk to. Jason had always been a good friend, but we stepped over the line a couple of times before I realized I wanted to save my marriage as did he."

The woman's confession pulled on Gabriella's heartstrings. "But Kyle is his son. What if he's more like Jason than he thinks he is?"

"*My* son has done everything in his power to be nothing like Jason, but understand, Jason can be an upstanding guy, when he pulls his head out of his pants."

Gabriella bit her lip at the woman's commentary. "When he talks of his father, he only mentioned Patrick. Always favorably. Always, lovingly."

Her eyes glistened. "If I could have cloned Patrick, I would have gotten no one better than Kyle. Not now, not in a million years. He's Patrick in almost every way, but to be fair, Patrick had his flaws. Pride was certainly one of them."

The way she stressed *almost* hurt Gabriella's heart. The loss of this one man had wounded all of them. "Kyle misses his dad terribly. I can hear it in his voice…and yours."

The corner of her mouth curled up. "My son is right to love you. You're fiercely protective of family. I can see it in your eyes. When I talk to your brothers, sisters, parents."

That comment came out of left field. "Oh, Lord. You talked to my parents?"

She tapped the rim of her coffee mug. "You might want to fill it up. Your family gave me an earful."

Chapter Twenty-Seven

WHAT AM I doing here?

Kyle stood outside Gabriella's front door but didn't knock.

He didn't know if he should, but he needed to see her. Being without her these past few days, he'd been lost. His heart ached, but he didn't deserve her.

As he turned to leave, the creak of the door stopped him in his tracks.

"You just gonna stand on my porch all day like some guy from a John Hughes movie?"

Turning, he sucked in a breath. Her natural beauty almost brought him to his knees.

A slight smile on her face, she motioned for him to enter. "Come on. Sit down. You're here for a reason."

He followed her to the kitchen without question as his gut twisted and the bitter taste of regret coated the back of his tongue.

Gabriella placed a mug, saucer, and spoon in front of a chair and filled the mug with coffee. "Sit down."

"Thanks."

Trinity began to pack her sketching supplies, but Gabriella motioned for her to stay. Her forehead furrowed, but she sat back down.

Holding the mug in his hands, he said nothing. He had no idea where to start.

Sitting next to him, she placed her hand on his arm. "Talk."

"Right after the trip Patrick and I took here, he was diagnosed with leukemia." The strength in his voice faltered. "He was a candidate for bone marrow transplant. Of course all of us kids were tested, to see if we were a match. Everyone decently matched, but I didn't match. I *really* didn't match."

"That sucks," Trinity blurted out, then slapped her hand over her mouth, giving a muffled, "Sorry."

"You're right, T. It sucked."

Pulling his hand to her heart, Gabriella sweetly encouraged, "That's how you found out? How old were you?"

"Fourteen."

"What a terrible way to find out. I'm so sorry."

The grip on her fingers slightly tightened. "I remember sitting in the waiting room, hearing my parents screaming at each other. I kept thinking, 'What could they be fighting about right now? We're in a hospital.'" He didn't move, but continued to sit, staring at his coffee mug. "Somebody at the hospital leaked the results to the press, then Mom confessed everything to a family friend. The friend turned around and did an interview for some scandal sheet."

"I can't believe someone would sell out their friend," Trinity mumbled.

"You'd be surprised what people will do for money. Press." He ran his finger along the rim of his cup. "When that made the papers, the shit hit the fan. Jason's wife divorced him and did plenty of interviews about the ugly of it."

"As if your family needed anything else to deal with." Tentatively, she rested her hand on his arm. "What happened to your parents?"

"They stayed together. Worked through it, but I don't think he ever made complete peace with her. Or me."

"Why you?" Trinity's lips went thin as she patted his back. "You didn't do anything wrong."

The still subtle anger in his father's eyes replayed in his mind. "I was a reminder of a time when they both failed each other."

"Still, you didn't do anything wrong."

"That right," Gabriella added. "You didn't."

The more he spoke, the weight of the words fell off him. For the first time in a long time, his past didn't hold the tight grip of regret around his brain or his soul. Looking up at Gabriella, he expected pity, but when he locked eyes with her, all he saw was love.

Pure unconditional love.

"I'm sorry I didn't trust you enough to tell you everything."

She cupped his face. "I understand why you didn't, but let's not make a habit of that."

"I'd like that." He pulled her into his arms. "I love you, Gabriella Marcos, and I want to spend the rest of my life not lying to you about anything."

"I would love that. And I love you, back."

Trinity jumped up and excitedly clapped her hands. "How cool!"

Holding his arm out, he pulled the teen into their hug. "And you too, T."

Cookie cat ran in and jumped on the table as Belle leaned against their group, her wagging tail hitting his leg.

He laughed at the chaos of it as the peace of having a family finally settled into his soul.

Epilogue

THE GRAFF HOTEL had never seen such an event before.

The Men of Marietta Calendar guys, plus Duke, stood near the front of the beautifully decorated grand ballroom as the press, including celebrity reporters from *Entertainment Tonight*, *Extra*, *Today Show*, *Vanity Fair*, and *Cosmo* peppered them with questions, until Charlie Foster stepped in and worked as moderator.

Despite the chaos, Kyle could easily see Gabriella and Trinity near his poster-sized print.

Around the ballroom, each of the months had been strategically arranged to encourage traffic to all of those who'd donated their time and bodies for the benefit of Harry's House.

In the last month, the weather had warmed enough to thaw the ground and they'd been able to take care of the drainage and foundation issues a week shy of their deadline.

As of tomorrow, Harry's House would officially be open and serving the kids of Marietta and surrounding counties.

"Kyle! Kyle!" One reporter waved his hand.

Charlie pointed. "Last question, folks."

The man stood and crossed his arms over his chest. "You took a big hiatus from the Hollywood lifestyle."

"If you call serving in our country's military and then fighting fires for this community a hiatus, I'd hate to know what you call a vacation."

A low rumble of laughter filled the room.

Kyle smirked, but the reporter's forehead furrowed deeper. "What about your family's business? What are your plans now that you've come back?"

Gabriella's eyes met his and she gave him a wink.

He found this situation ironic since he'd done everything to avoid any press, but today, he couldn't be more than happy to announce his news. "I plan to stay in Marietta for a good long time, raise a family."

"No plans to return to Hollywood and follow in your famous *father*'s footsteps?" The sharp indignation in the man's voice could have cut glass. "Or your mother's and manage one of the family's hotels?"

He shook his head. He still didn't like the press, and he wouldn't play this game. Not today. "No, my life is here. I've got a good life with good people. One of whom we're honoring with the money we've raised from this calendar."

The reporter's forehead furrowed. "Yes, but—"

"Today isn't about anyone but Harry Monroe. The man who left us too soon, but will live forever helping the kids of this community."

The other men nodded and applauded, which stirred

everyone else to do the same.

"You silk-tongued bastard," Brett whispered as he slapped Kyle on the back. "That was brilliant."

"Thank you for coming, everybody." Charlie waved her hands as the men found their families and significant others.

Walking up to a smiling Gabriella, Kyle's heart raced.

As soon as he arrived, Freddie walked up, his hands shoved in his pockets. "Hey, Trinity."

"Freddie!" She threw her arms around him and he hugged her back but dropped his arms as soon as he made eye contact with Kyle.

"Thanks for being here." Kyle pulled Gabriella into his arms.

She kissed his cheek. "I wouldn't miss it."

"Mom, can Freddie and I go to Java Café?"

With a nod, Gabriella replied, "Yes, but meet us at Harry's House by four. We want to be there for the ribbon cutting."

As the kids walked away, Kyle glanced at the large picture of himself and cringed. "Now what are they going to do with that after all this is over?"

"I don't know, but it really doesn't matter."

"Oh, yeah? Why's that?"

She smiled up at him. "Because I have the real thing."

"You sure as hell do."

The End

The Marietta Medical Series

Book 1: Resisting the Doctor

The Men of Marietta series

When there isn't enough money to make Harry's House a functional afterschool center, the Montana First Responders decide they need to step up, and really turn up the heat. The Men of Marietta Calendar is created with pages filled of sexy guys willing to do just about anything for a great cause....

Book 1: *Tempting the Deputy* by Heidi Rice

Book 2: *Flirting with Fire* by Kate Hardy

Book 3: *Daring the Pilot* by Jeannie Moon

Book 4: *Falling for the Ranger* by Kaylie Newell

Book 5: *Burning with Desire* by Patricia W. Fischer

About the Author

Native Texan Patricia W. Fischer is a natural-born storyteller. Ever since she listened to her great-grandmother tell stories about her upbringing in the early 1900s, Patricia has been hooked on hearing of great adventures and love winning in the end.

On her way to becoming an award-winning writer, she became a percussionist, actress, singer, waitress, bartender, pre-cook, and finally a trauma nurse before she realized she needed to get her butt to a journalism class.

After earning her journalism degree from Washington University, Patricia has been writing for multiple publications on numerous subjects including women's health, foster/adoption advocacy, ovarian cancer education, and entertainment features.

These days she spends her days with her family, two dogs, and a few fish while she creates a good story with a touch of reality, a dash of laughter, and a whole lot of love.

Visit her at PatriciaWFischer.com

Thank you for reading

Burning with Desire

If you enjoyed this book, you can find more from all our great authors at TulePublishing.com, or from your favorite online retailer.

Made in the USA
Columbia, SC
24 June 2024